A Slave of Catiline

High School & Junior Collgee List

Abbott, F. F.:   The Common People of Ancient Rome
Anderson, P. L.:   A Slave of Catiline
Anderson, P. L.:   For Freedom and for Gaul
Anderson, P: L.:   Pugnax, the Gladiator
Anderson, P. L.:   Swords in the North
Anderson, P. L.:   With the Eagles
Cheney, D.:   Son of Minos
Church, A. J.:   Lucius
Church, A. J.:   Roman Life in the Days of Cicero
Davis, W. S.:   A Day in Old Athens
Davis, W. S.:   A Day in Old Rome
Donauer, F.:   Swords Against Carthage
Judson, H. P.:   Caesar's Army
Lamprey, L.:   Children of Ancient Gaul
Lamprey, L.:   Children of Ancient Rome
Mayer, A. I. Jr.:   Olympiad
Wells, R. F.:   On Land and Sea with Caesar
Wells, R. F.:   With Caesar's Legions
White, J. S.:   Plutarch's "Lives"
Whitehead, A. C.:   The Standard Bearer

I CAST MY NET

[page 48]

A Slave of Catiline

BY

Paul L. Anderson

Illustrated by
Norman L. Roberts

BIBLO and TANNEN

ISBN: 0-8196-0101-2

WITH AFFECTIONATE REGARD

THIS BOOK IS INSCRIBED TO

MY VALUED FRIEND OF MANY YEARS' STANDING

THE ORATOR, STATESMAN, AND PATRIOT

MARCUS TULLIUS CICERO

CONTENTS

ILLUSTRATIONS

CHAPTER I

Of the Coming of the Pirates; and How I Was Sold for a Gladiator

"TO the hills! To the hills! The pirates are at hand! It is Gaza's ship!"

The ever-dreaded cry rang through the village, and out from cabin and hut there poured a frightened crowd, the men hastily girding on their swords, the women carrying what possessions they could lay quick hands on and urging their terrified children to greater speed. Stark fear gripped every one; these pirate raids were not uncommon along our coast, and they left behind them a trail of misery, of slaughtered men, looted cabins, villages in flames, and men and women and children of all ages carried from their homes to be sold in the slave-marts of Delos or Rome or Alexandria. And Gaza and his associate, Sportella, were known far and wide as the most ruthless, the most utterly merciless, of all the savage Cilicians who infested the shores of the Mare Internum.* I take it that these were assumed names, Gaza being the Persian word for riches, while Sportella of course signifies the little basket

* The Mediterranean.

I

in which a wealthy patron hands out the daily dole of food to his clients. But whether real or false, they were of evil omen, and we tarried not a moment in our flight.

I had been engaged with my foster-father in mending our fishing-nets, but at the first shout we dropped our work, rushed into the hut, and seized our arms. He grasped his sword, and I took mine from the peg on which it hung, but in addition I took a stout bow—my favorite weapon—and a quiver of arrows. My foster-mother snatched up a loaf of bread, a bit of cheese, and a couple of dried fish, called to her daughter Polla, a maid of some thirteen years, and the four of us joined the ragged line of fugitives who sought safety in the hills.

The men cursing bitterly or grimly silent, the women shrieking their terror to the sky, the children sobbing and wailing their dread of they knew not what awful fate, so the pushing, jostling crowd streamed out in flight. A few of us kept our heads, helped on the weaker ones, watched over the fear-mad wretches, formed ourselves into a rear-guard. We knew that on our return we would find our homes in ashes, but what was that compared to death or—far worse—the auction-block and the bitter bread of slavery? Glancing back as I topped the first little rise, a half mile or so inland from our village, I saw the bireme of Gaza draw into our bay, its purple sails fluttering down as it lost its motion. Well, we had been warned in time; before the pirates could land and overtake us we would be hidden among the sheltering caves and rocks. Far to the north I caught a glimpse of a white sail against the ocean's blue, and I murmured a prayer to Neptunus, ruler of the sea, that it might be one of Pompeius' galleys; that general had of late, as we had heard, done much against the pirates.

But from the leaders of the flight there rose a wail of despair, and before us we saw deployed a long line of armed men; Sportella had landed farther up the coast, marched down to the hills back of our village, and cut off our retreat. And in that moment I knew there was no hope of rescue; it was not a Roman galley that I had seen.

Then the women ran madly to and fro, shrieking more wildly than ever; loosened hair flying in the breeze, garments fluttering, silly hands waving in futile gestures or lifted to implore mercy of those hearts of bronze, they were run down by the swifter-footed pirates and bound hand and foot with quick sailor skill. As for the men—in truth, only the veriest craven will hold back from fighting when his loved ones are in peril, and without shame I can say that we did what we could. But how might we, without protective armor and with but casual weapons, stand against the well armed and disciplined men of Sportella? It was no ordered battle, but a furious mêlée of sword and dagger, spear and pike, and in the end, fighting desperately, we stretched some score of pirates dead or wounded on the ground. But we suffered five times the damage we wrought, and the destiny of battle was foreordained. As to myself, I saw three fall before my arrows, and with my sword I accounted for two more, but even as I pushed the last one off my blade something descended with a stunning crash upon my head, I pitched forward into a vast abyss of midnight dark and for me the fight was over.

I have spoken of my foster-father and foster-mother, and indeed, I had no recollection of my real parents. My earliest memory was of being tossed about on a vessel that rocked and pitched under a gray-black sky, and of a kind-faced man who spoke soothing words and lashed me to a block of timber. I remembered also being slid into the water, and my terror thereat, a terror that made me want to scream aloud, while at the same time my childish pride bade me choke back my cries. Thereafter, a gap in my recollections, but in later years I learned that in a great storm a Roman pleasure-yacht was driven ashore and that I was the only one who escaped the fury of the waves. The

The Coming of the Pirates

vessel broke up on the eastern coast of Italia, in the Mare Adriaticum, between Barium and Cannae; and the folk of a nameless village, hunting amid the wreck for salvage, found me, a child of four years, the only living creature of the ship's company. The wreckage was scattered far and wide along the shore, together with bodies of the crew, and there was nothing to tell whose was the yacht, or whence it came. Nor was there anything to show who I was save a gold *bulla* suspended about my neck by a chain, and on it the letters TIB, whence it was inferred that my parents had named me Tiberius. A certain fisherman had recently lost a child of about my age, and to his superstitious mind it seemed that Father Neptunus had sent me to replace his dead son, so he promptly adopted me and I grew up in his home, being variously known in the village as Tiberius or—from the color of my hair—Rufus. About a year after the wreck the fisherman's wife gave birth to a daughter, and Polla and I grew up as brother and sister, nor could any have told, from the treatment accorded us, that we were not of the same blood; my foster-parents were uniformly kind to me, and treated me like their own son. Of course, I was early put to work, but this represented no harshness; the living we got from the sea was by no means plentiful, and everyone must do what he was able. However, my tasks were suited to my strength, and I believe they helped rather than hindered my growth and the development of muscle and agility which later brought me some reputation and saved my life over and over again.

But if life in our village was hard, it was in the main peaceful. We went in dread of pirate raids, to be sure, but except for this we were untouched by battle or striving. Rumors came to us from time to time of fierce political warfare in the City, of conspiracy, proscription, and bitter struggles for power, but these things passed us by, nor did they disturb the quiet progress of our days. And I would have laughed in disbelief had some seer or prophet told me that I was destined to play no small part in the deadliest and most desperate of all the conspiracies that ever tortured our mighty State.

Growing older, I went with my foster-father on his voyages, helping him cast and draw his nets, and venturing with him to the coast of Illyricum or round the southern cape to Syracusae, Messana, or Rhegium, and once as far north as Baiae. And now, fourteen years after the wreck, in the year DCLXXXIX A.U.C.*, I was a tall and well-grown youth of eighteen, already as strong as many men, and able to pull an oar or haul a net or manage a boat with any in the village.

But it seemed that my fishing days were over, for

* 65 B.C.

when I regained my senses I found myself manacled hand and foot, and from the tossing of the rough planks on which I lay I knew that I was in the hold of a ship at sea. It was black as the nethermost pit of the realm of Dis, and in truth I thought at first that I had died and gone to Pluto's kingdom, for my head ached sickeningly, my throat was parched and my tongue swollen from thirst, and all about me I could hear groans and wails of agony, the sobbing of children, and the retching of miserable creatures overtaken by that worst of all maladies, the sickness of the waves. Gradually, however, my head cleared, the pain grew less, and I understood what had happened; that the raid was successful, and that I was one of this unhappy company bound for the slave-market and the auction-block.

Unlike many biremes, Gaza's was decked over fore and aft to make a prison, so that whether by night or by day no glimmer of light reached us, and we could not tell the passage of the days. But from time to time sundry of our captors moved about among us with torches, bringing a scanty dole of bread and water and herding us around with kicks and blows and curses, and from these visits I was able to form some estimate of time. On the eighth day, as nearly as I could judge, we were ordered on deck, and shuffling in the chains that bound our feet, we obeyed, coming out into a blaze of light that smote our unaccustomed eyes with all the force of a blow. Adjusting my sight, I looked around, to see all about us the intense blue of the Mare Internum, and off to eastward a white-sailed ship—Sportella's. To westward I could descry the masts and towering marbles of Syracusae, from which port a small sailing-vessel came dancing toward us over the waves. We were hove to, and she drew even with us, heaving to likewise and putting over a small boat that was rowed swiftly to our side, from which boat there climbed over our bulwarks a figure such as I had never before seen.

He was a man of medium size, dressed in a once-white woollen tunic and red leather sandals; his hair descended in glistening oily ringlets to his slightly stooped shoulders, and over his bosom there spread a curly, greasy beard that bore unmistakable traces of food; and to complete the picture, both his clothes and his person were of an utterly incredible filthiness, though on his fingers glittered several brilliant jewels. I could not make out whether he was Greek, Syrian, or Jew, but in any case Chiron—for so Gaza called him—was unwholesome enough to disgrace any country. He addressed the pirates with unctuous courtesy, speaking to the two leaders cringingly yet with an odd suggestion of boldness, as though his respect were more a politic outward showing than a genuine feeling; and Sportella bellowed an order to his men to draw us up in lines along the deck. While we shuffled to our places I looked about among the prisoners, some two hundred in all, fruit of more than one raid, but could see nothing of my foster-parents; I learned afterward that they had both been slain. Polla I did catch sight of, and nodded and smiled encouragingly to her; it went to my heart to see her pretty face streaked with tears and drawn with misery.

But now we were ranged in line, and Chiron, with Gaza and Sportella, marched along inspecting us. Sportella was a big man, huge of frame and heavily muscled, with round red face and booming voice, yet for all his bulk he deferred to the smaller but more deadly Gaza, who, with his straggly hair and moustache and his coldly cruel face, reminded me of some venomous spider. The inspection over, Chiron asked:

"Shall I bid on them one by one, or in the herd?"

"One by one," answered Sportella, but Gaza contradicted him, saying:

"In the herd."

"After all, that would be better," amended Sportella. "Yes, in the herd, Chiron, in the herd."

"There are some that are of no use to me," said Chiron, and Gaza replied:

9

"Point them out."

The slave-dealer indicated eight men and three women, bent and broken with years, and Gaza called an order to his men:

"Overboard with them."

"Shall we strike off their chains?" asked one of the pirates, and Gaza snarled:

"No! Do we want them swimming and squalling about the ship?"

And the eleven unfortunates, despite their screams and pleadings for mercy, were dragged to the bulwarks and incontinently tossed into the sea, where they sank at once.

I was sick with horror at this brutal callousness, but Chiron, unmoved, had been performing some mental arithmetic, and now he announced:

"There are a hundred and seventy-eight; twenty *denarii* apiece; three thousand five hundred *denarii** for the lot, landed at Tiber wharf."

"*Per Deos Immortales!*" howled Sportella. "Twenty *denarii* apiece! And you will average two *sestertia*† apiece—perchance more."

"For some," replied Chiron, deprecatingly. "For others, less."

"And landed at Tiber wharf! *Di bene vortant!*" And with extended fore and little fingers he made

---

*$612.50. A *denarius* was 17½ cents.
†A *sestertium* was about $43.

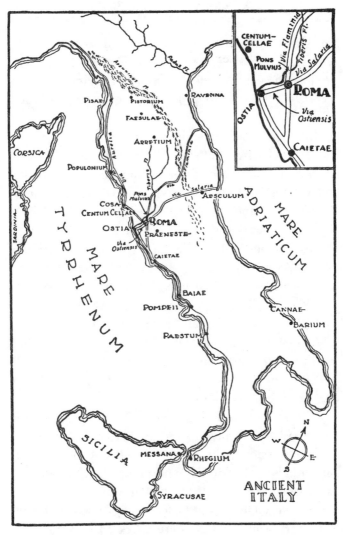

ANCIENT ITALY, SHOWING THE PLACES MENTIONED
IN THE STORY

the sign of the horns, to ward off evil fortune. "Do you think we seek the cross? We will land them at Paestum, but no nearer Rome—Pompeius is too active and too ready to crucify gentlemen of our trade."

Chiron bowed and rubbed his hands.

"In that case," he said, "the price will be fifteen *denarii* a head. Not a few would die on the march from Paestum to Rome, and some would slay themselves or escape."

"Any that escape you—!" boomed Sportella. "And do you think to dictate terms to us, you filthy *mango?* You greasy-whiskered, foul-smelling, blood-sucking scum of the Alexandrian gutters—"

"Enough!" broke in Gaza's cold voice.

"But—" and Sportella turned to his associate.

"Enough! Chiron, we will land them at Ostia, and you will pay us six thousand *denarii* for the lot."

"But, most noble sir—" began Chiron, only to be cut off by Gaza with:

"You heard me! Thus will there be ample profit for you; take it, or I throw the herd to the waves."

"Very well, noble sir," responded Chiron, humbly, and betook himself to his boat, while the pirates, at a word from Gaza, got under way.

We were landed at Ostia, our leg-irons and bracelets were removed, we were shackled neck to neck, and Chiron and half a dozen of his servants started us on the fourteen-mile march from Tiber mouth to Rome.

For me it was an easy enough journey, but difficult for some of the weaker ones, and the *lorarii* plied the lash freely ere we caught our first glimpse of the City of Quirinus. But when we did come within view of that mighty City, towering on its seven hills, the white marble stucco of the patrician homes on the Palatine glowing warm in the sun of late afternoon, for a moment I forgot my weariness, forgot that I was a wretched slave, and stood lost in awe and wonder. I have since learned that the approach along the Via Ostiensis does not give so fine a view of Rome as the approaches on the other side of the City, namely, the Via Tiburtina and the Via Flaminia, but at that time the City housed more than half a million souls, and any aspect of it was impressive enough to a fisher lad who knew no place larger than Syracusae. And when to this were added all the stories and traditions of Rome's greatness, small wonder that I stood and stared until the biting whip reminded me that I was no longer my own man, but had been sold as one of a herd, like some lowly bullock.

We entered through the Porta Ostiensis, marched along the Vicus Tuscus, skirted to the south of the Forum, where we saw on our left, above the shops and other buildings, the Temple of Jupiter Capitolinus, and so into the Subura, a place of narrow streets, tall tenements, and evil stenches. Eye-filling marvels were all about us, and not least of them the height of the Suburan buildings, for though the palaces of the patricians never rise more than two stories, and often only one, these rickety frame tenements tower five and six and even seven floors above the street. Into a dark, damp, and reeking cellar under one of these we were thrust, our neck-irons were removed and our ankles once more shackled, we were given a loaf of bread and a pitcher of water apiece, and there we were left in obscurity to wonder what the coming day had in store.

In this noisome hole we remained for six days, awaiting the date set by the aedile—the magistrate in charge of such affairs—for the public auction; then early one morning our guards roused us and drove us out and back the way we had come until we reached the Forum Boarium, the cattle-market near the Porta Flumentana. The open space was more or less crowded with cattle, together with buyers and sellers, and the stalls about the sides were full, but at one end a place had been cleared, the block set up, and all preparations for the auction were complete. Two other slave-dealers besides Chiron had arrived to offer their wares, and as we marched in their gangs drew near, coming from the other side of the market, until there were at least five hundred men, women, and children to be sold. It did not seem to me that all could be sold in one day, and in truth I was right, for other like sales that I afterward attended consumed several days. But now a crier mounted the stand beside the block and barked an announcement, whereat a number of those loitering about the market turned and drew near. The crier stepped down, to be replaced by the auctioneer, and the sale began.

Most of the slaves to be sold had their feet whitened with chalk, in token that they were newly imported and that the customs duty had been paid, and of these practically none had scrolls of guarantee hung about their necks, but were sold with a cap on their heads as a sign that the dealer gave no warrant of health or character with them. Of those with unwhitened feet, however, almost all were guaranteed; they were being sold, for one reason or another, by private owners. I saw blacks from Nubia, Greeks of evident education and refinement, uncouth barbarians from the North, sharp-featured and dark-skinned men and women from Egypt— people of ever   and nation, until it seemed that all the world   ..u been laid under tribute to furnish slaves to Rome. I caught sight of my sister Polla, but she was too far away for me to speak to her, though I did manage to catch her eye and throw her a smile and a nod.

It chanced that I stood near the block, and I was able in some measure to forget my wretchedness in listening to the comments of the crowd that pressed close about us and to the patter of the auctioneer, and in admiring the clever way in which he coaxed up the bidding. But I felt my cheeks grow hot with vicarious shame when the first woman was offered for sale. She was a young Greek of perhaps twenty years, with a gentle and refined face and a charming figure; her garments were expensive though now torn and soiled; and she gazed about her with a wondering look in which fear and grief played no small part. It seemed that she could not understand the Latin tongue, for when told to step up on the block she only stared blankly; and when one of Chiron's men grasped her arm and thrust her forward she shrank from him in dread. But when she realized what was wanted she mounted with docility, and it.was plain that her appearance attracted attention, for there was a stir of interest among the crowd.

"She will make a good *vestiplica* for me," commented a fat, red-faced man in the toga of a curule magistrate. "The one I have now grows lazy, and I am sending her to my farm."

"No *vestiplica* could make a toga lie in graceful folds over that paunch of yours, my Lentulus," laughed a patrician dame, tapping him playfully on the arm with her fan. "Better let me have her for a hair-dresser."

"I wonder if she is educated," another bejeweled woman remarked. She spoke to the girl in some language that I did not know, though I took it to be Greek, for I caught the word *"Homeros."*

The slave's face brightened, and she replied at length in the same flowing tongue, whereat the woman nodded as though satisfied. Other questions were asked and answered, then the first woman spoke to the auctioneer.

"Is she sound of limb and in good health?"

The man smiled and responded:

"She is sold *sine titulo*. But you can inspect her."

He nodded to two of his assistants, and stepping forward they laid hands on the girl's clothing. As though warned by instinct, she tried to protect herself, but one of them caught and held her wrists while the other stripped off her garments, leaving her naked before the crowd. With a little cry, she buried her face in her hands and tried to turn her back to the multitude, but was dragged around and made to lift her head and to face the people while the patrician dame pinched and poked her, felt of her limbs, and satisfied herself as to the girl's condition, even having her hair unbound, to judge its length and thickness. For myself, I was furious at such indignity laid on a girl of good birth, and when the men first stripped her I started involuntarily forward to protect her. But my shackles tripped me, and as I picked myself up amid the laughter of the crowd I realized how futile such an effort would be; realized, too, that we were no longer human beings, but merely cattle; and I stood silent though raging in my place. Nor did it help my mood to know that Polla would undoubtedly be given the same brutal treatment.

The girl was quickly knocked down, being sold, after some brisk bidding, to the woman who had asked about her education; twelve *sestertia* was the price paid, a most unusual figure; however, captives of her quality were rare and brought good sums. She was allowed to dress and was led away weeping, and the sale continued.

At length it came my turn, and I mounted the block, removing my clothes when ordered; in truth, after the adventures of the past fortnight I had but little left to remove.

"Here, now," said the auctioneer, "is a strong, sound, tall, well-formed youth, as you can see for yourselves. He would make a good litter-bearer, or he would last long at the mill or in the quarry. Who will start the bidding? What am I offered? Do I hear ten *sestertia?*"

"Two *sestertia*," called the woman who had bought the Greek.

"Three!" cried another, in a different part of the crowd. "It is my fancy to have a full set of red-haired litter-bearers, and I already have six. Three *sestertia.*"

"Does he know anything of swordsmanship?" shouted a burly, yellow-haired, blue-eyed man, and the auctioneer turned to me, repeating the question.

I thought of the pirates whom I had slain, and smiled a trifle grimly as I replied:

"Ask of Sportella's men."

"*Per Martes!*" laughed a soldier. "If that is needful to answer you, Dumnorix, then shall you never know."

"Why not?" boomed the giant.

"Have you not heard? Four days since, Pompeius overtook Gaza and Sportella off Caieta and adorned some two hundred crosses with what was left of their men after the fighting was over. They dared too greatly when they landed this herd at Ostia."

"The Gods give them peace," said Dumnorix. "They were brave men. Three and a half."

I whispered to an attendant standing near:

"Who is the big man?"

"Dumnorix," he answered. "A *lanista.*"

"A *lanista?* What is that?" For the word was new to me.

The attendant glanced at me curiously.

19

"Whence do you come, barbarian? From some coast town, by your speech. He is a trainer of gladiators for the arena—as you will learn if he bids you in."

"Four!" shouted someone else.

The first woman shook her head when the auctioneer glanced at her, but the second nodded, and he said:

"Four and a half I am offered. Who will make it five? Will you?" This to the magistrate.

The latter shook his head.

"My urban family is complete," he answered. "And it is too much for a farm slave."

"Five!" bellowed Dumnorix.

The dame nodded again.

"Five and a half I am offered. Who will make it six? Do I hear six? No? Shame on the Roman people, to let a handsome and sturdy youth go for such a price! Dumnorix, your gladiators have brought you many a good purse; surely you can afford six *sestertia* to add another to their list. Think of all the good gold he will earn for you in the arena!"

"Aye!" answered the *lanista*. "If he be not slain in his tyro bout! Well—Pluto seize you!—six."

The auctioneer turned to the woman who was bidding on me.

"Will you forego your red-haired litter-bearer

for a mere half *sestertium, Domina?* If I remember correctly, he would match well with the others in size, would he not? And then you will need but one to complete the tale. Will you say six and a half?"

"My man vowed that if I paid more than five he would sell them all—but I can talk him over. So be it!"

The crowd cheered and laughed, while Dumnorix' hard face flushed with anger.

"*Habet!*" cried someone. "Dumnorix has it!" It was the cry that greets a vanquished gladiator. and the *lanista* grew still redder.

"*Non habeo!*" he cried. "I have not got it. Seven!"

By now the crowd was cheering both contestants, and the woman glanced angrily about, biting her lip.

"And a half!" she called.

"Eight!" boomed the Gaul.

"And a half!"

Suddenly Dumnorix jumped his bid.

"Ten!" he shouted, and the spectators howled with delight.

The woman shook her head at the auctioneer.

"The Gods blast you, Dumnorix!" she said. "But at least I have made you pay well for him."

"*Mehercle*, yes!" agreed the *lanista*, ruefully, now

that the heat of strife had left him. "Twice what he is worth. Well, it is a gamble, and we live by taking chances. Pluto have mercy on him if I lose money by my bargain!"

He paid over the money, then turned to me.

"Come along, you. Put on your tunic. What is your name?"

"Tiberius."

"Come along, then, Tiberius. And Mars hear me, if you do not earn me your price I will pay the priests of Cybele to lay a curse on you in the next world."

He started off, I shuffling behind him, but before we had gone more than a few paces I stopped him.

"Domine," I begged, "may I ask a favor?"

"What is it?" he growled.

"My sister Polla is to be sold to-day. Would you not buy her also, that we may not be separated?"

He stared at me.

"In the name of Mars!" he exploded. "When I have paid such a price for you? And what would a girl be doing in a stable of gladiators? If she is a good girl it would be a living death, and if she is not I would not have her there. My darlings have other tools than distaff and needle!"

"Then you will not?"

"Per Martes!" he grunted, and resumed his swaggering march.

The Coming of the Pirates

Heartsick, I fell in behind, and followed him to the barrack which was to be my home for two long years, where the Gods had destined me to know both hope and despair, both joy and misery unspeakable, until it was Their good pleasure to set me free from that hell of savage men.

CHAPTER II

Of the Gladiators' Barrack; and My Fight with Pugnax

I SOON found that Dumnorix was more than a mere trainer of gladiators; he was owner, manager, and match-maker as well, and got his living by renting out our strength and skill either to the State or to those private individuals who wished, being candidates for office, to make themselves popular by giving free games. The barrack to which he led me was a huge, rambling structure only a short walk from the cattle-market, being at the lower end of the Campus Martius, just outside the Porta Flumentana; that is, in the V formed by the City wall and Tiber bank. The building was about twenty feet in height, of stucco-faced masonry and roofed with red tiles; and there were no windows in the outer walls. As I came to know the City better I learned that the finer homes had but few outer windows, and in this respect we were one with the dwellers on the Palatine, though not for the same reason—Dumnorix was taking no chances of an escape, the revolt of Spartacus being still fresh in Roman minds. A single door of heavy timber faced us as we approached, and on this Dumnorix thundered with the hilt of his sword. There was a barred opening a foot or so square in the door, and in response to the summons there showed here an evil, scarred face, with the left eyelid drooped over an empty socket; the other eye inspected us, then a grin spread over the face, and with rattling of bolts the door swung back to let us enter. The *janitor* was a burly man, armed with sword and dagger, and fastened to the wall by a chain some ten or twelve feet long.

"Ho, Scelus," said Dumnorix, "here is another for the arena. See that he does not escape."

"Small chance!" rumbled the other, eyeing me appraisingly. "He is a goodly youth; does he know aught of swordplay?"

"That we shall learn. Is Marcus within?"

"Aye." The *janitor* closed and barred the door, and Dumnorix, nodding, strode on through the vestibule, I at his heels.

I found myself in a roofless earth-floored court some twenty-five by thirty-five paces*, around whose four sides ran a colonnade; the columns supported a balcony, on which opened a number of rooms, corner stairways giving access to these; and in the shade under the balcony I could make out other doors. All in all, there were nearly a hundred rooms, most

*The Roman pace was a double stride of five feet in length.

of them about twelve feet square and serving as sleeping chambers, though some larger ones were used as armory, offices, guard-room, baths, and kitchen. I may say here that Dumnorix maintained an excellent kitchen, also a very complete bathing establishment, the latter having steam room, hot and cold rooms, showers, plunge, and two most skillful masseurs.

In one angle of the court a man was sitting on the ground with his feet thrust through two holes in a plank, and he strove to defend himself against another who was beating him about the head with a dead cat, while a dozen or so more looked on and roared with laughter.

"He is in the stocks for insubordination," Dumnorix explained. "It is the custom that when a man is so punished the others may torment him in any way they see fit, provided they do him no actual harm."

In the center of the exercise ground several pairs of men, fully armed, fenced with wooden swords, and off to one side another heavily armed man fenced with one who, carrying only a net and a trident, strove to throw the net over his adversary and entangle him in its folds. Two others, seated on benches, watched the fencers keenly, calling admonition and advice to them, and still others, standing about, greeted each hit with laughter and jeers.

The Gladiators' Barrack

Realizing that I would soon be doing something of this nature, I looked on with interest, but Dumnorix let out a bellow:

"Marcus! Glaucus! Aesculapius!"

One of the men on the benches rose and sauntered toward us; a scarred, muscular, hard-faced man he was, victor, as I was told later, in more than a hundred fights in the arena, and now retired and serving as teacher of gladiators.

"Marcus," said my owner, "here is a tyro; provide him with arms and find out if he knows aught of weapons."

The teacher grunted a surly assent and looked me over, and two others, emerging from rooms on the ground floor, drew near. One of them was the most horrible creature I had ever seen, fat, bloated, coarse and brutal of countenance, and scarred from innumerable sword-cuts; the other, who wore a long gray beard flowing down over his tunic, was grave and kindly, with the brow of a philosopher, and seemed strangely out of place in such a den of beasts. I learned later that he and Marcus were the only free men in the school.

"Glaucus," Dumnorix told the gross man, "strike off these leg-irons. And do you, Aesculapius, look him over and tell me if he is sound."

The bearded man forthwith gave me a most thorough examination, from which, together with

27

his name, I inferred that he was a physician whom Dumnorix employed to care for the health of the gladiators, and to tend such wounded men as were not slain in the arena. By the time I was pronounced sound and healthy, Glaucus, working with chisel and hammer and bar, had cut my shackles off, whereupon Marcus gave me helmet, shield, and wooden sword; he himself wore no defensive armor, merely taking a sword like mine.

"Now, boy," he said, "show us what you can do. Defend yourself, and lay on hard; fear not to strike."

For perhaps quarter of an hour I did my best, but not once did I get home with blow or thrust; Marcus seemed to know beforehand what I intended, and turned my sword with utter ease. And he hit or prodded me at will, until my shoulder and sides and legs were sore and my head rang; to do him justice, though, he was not unduly harsh; it was merely that we were playing a rough game.

"Enough!" he called at length, and turned to Dumnorix. "He knows nothing whatever."

"So I see," answered the *lanista,* dryly. "I have made a bad bargain. Ten *sestertia* he cost me."

Marcus whistled.

"Ten *sestertia,* eh? It is a good price. How came you to pay it?"

"Fulvia bid me up, Pluto seize her! Yes, a bad bargain."

Marcus considered.

"No, I would not say that," he told the other. "It is a good price, indeed, for a tyro. But he is sound and strong, and I like the look in his eye and his general bearing. It is in my mind—" He broke off and turned to me. "Run twice around the colonnade as swiftly as you can," he ordered.

I obeyed, returning to the group, and Marcus nodded.

"He is in good condition," he said. "See, after all that fencing and the run he is barely sweating and is not winded. And he is agile and swift. He would do better as a *retiarius* than heavy-armed; further, his being left-handed will give him an advantage."

Dumnorix grunted, then told Glaucus to show me to my quarters and give me clothes.

"Put him in with Murena," he said, and Glaucus led me to a room in the upper tier.

Like all the bedrooms, this was furnished with two cots, two chairs, and several wall pegs for garments. Some of the gladiators had chests in which to keep favorite weapons or other possessions, but none of the rooms was exactly palatial. Glaucus brought in a coarse woollen tunic, undergarments, and sandals, tossed them on the bed, and jerked his thumb over his shoulder, growling:

"Dinner in two hours. Bath-rooms in that corner, downstairs." And forthwith he left me to my own devices.

Considering that a bath would not come amiss, since I had accumulated plenty of dirt and vermin in Gaza's ship and Chiron's cellar, I took my new clothing and made my way to the baths. It was a novel experience for me, who had hitherto done all my bathing in the ocean, to go through the sweat-room, the showers, and the plunge, and to be massaged and oiled from head to foot, and I enjoyed it thoroughly. Being a tyro, of course I had to wait for the older gladiators, and I occupied the time in listening to their conversation, which, however, I did not find very edifying; it dealt almost entirely with fighting, drinking, women, and gambling. My foster-parents were poor, it is true, but they were decent folk, and I now heard much talk that shocked my unaccustomed ears. But I had sense enough to realize that the life these men led, being one of brutality and danger, must necessarily make them coarse and cruel in their amusements as in their work; that only those who were hard of mind and of body could survive; and I quickly decided that for my own protection I must put on a shell of seeming hardness. The Gods be thanked, though, that I never grew to be inwardly hard.

Refreshed by the bath, and comfortable in my clean garments, I sought the dining-tables, which were set in the open air, under the colonnade. Here Dumnorix introduced me to the others with a wave of his hand, saying merely:

"Tiberius, a tyro. Murena, he sleeps with you."

Murena, a heavy-set, not unpleasant looking youth of my own age, shook hands with me and spoke a word of greeting, and we lay down to our meal.

Dumnorix had unusual notions in the matter of feeding his gladiators—rather, the ideas were those of Aesculapius, who had convinced Dumnorix of their worth. Most of the *lanistae* fed their men chiefly meat, and that almost raw, to make them fierce; gave them huge quantities of wine; and encouraged them to stuff themselves. Dumnorix did exactly the reverse. He insisted on our eating largely of vegetables; he limited us to a pint of thrice-watered Etrurian wine to a meal; and if he saw one of his men growing fat, the unfortunate spent his mealtimes for two days in the stocks, going without food. It was unheard-of treatment, but I am bound to admit that we won more fights in the arena than did the men of any other *lanista,* and we were wholly free from the boils that so often afflicted

31

the other schools, so it may be that there was some thing in it after all.

Dinner being over, we rested for an hour or more, then the men who had not fenced during the morning had their practice, and I took my first lesson.

A *retiarius* wears no defensive armor, but only a kilt, light sandals, and a leather shoulder-guard, and his trident is simply the tool with which he brings down his entangled opponent; the real weapon is the net. This is made of medium stout cords, and is large enough to enmesh his adversary hopelessly, yet when gathered up it forms a light ball about the size of a man's head. It must be folded in a certain way, so that when cast from a distance of perhaps two paces it will spread out over the *secutor* and hamper him, and it has attached to it a light rope; this rope serves at once to aid the flip of the wrist which opens the net as it is thrown, and to give the *retiarius* a little start if he misses his cast and must gather the net while running away. My teacher was a little, wizen-faced, monkey-like man named Orontes, and he drilled me over and over and over again in the correct way of making the cast and of folding the net while running. And ever he demanded speed and yet more speed. Hour after hour and day after day we worked, sometimes just the two of us, sometimes several other tyro *retiarii* in the group, and at length Orontes declared me advanced enough to be matched against a *secutor*.

"Not in the arena, though,". he explained. "A good *secutor* would make sausage of you. In practice bouts only, for a while yet."

We were resting at the time, and I asked, idly:

"Why a *secutor*? Why not another *retiarius*?"

Orontes looked at me curiously.

"You have been here three months, and do not know that two *retiarii* are never matched? Your opponent will be heavy-armed; a Samnite, Thracian, or Gaul."

"Why?"

He shrugged.

"It is the custom."

"It sounds none too pleasant," I commented. "He with helmet, shield, and sword, and I with only my net and that foolish trident."

Orontes laughed.

"Do you see any scars on my face or body?" he asked. "Yet I have fought seventy-nine times in the arena. Half a dozen more fights, and I can buy my freedom and a little farm in Sabinum. The betting is commonly five to three or five to two on the *retiarius*. In truth, only a clumsy or careless netman has aught to fear."

"I can promise you," said I, fervently, "that whether clumsy or not, I will never be careless!"

Orontes laughed again.

"You are far from clumsy, my Tiberius," he assured me. "I look for you to do well on the sands."

All of which was at least encouraging.

Meanwhile, I had been settling down into my new life. Once my ears were pierced and ringed in token of slavery, I was accepted as one of the band, and had opportunity to become acquainted with the other gladiators, finding them a curious mixture of good and evil. There were from a hundred and fifty to two hundred in Dumnorix' school, for the number was continually varying; new ones were coming in, and some did not return from the arena. But whether young or old, tyro or veteran, they had two traits in common. The first of these I have already mentioned, their coarseness, with which were joined a hardness, a ferocity, and an indifference to pain—whether their own or another's —that made their play resemble the fighting of ordinary men. Fist-fights were common, and a favorite sport was cudgel-fighting, in which two men, stark naked, fought with sticks of ash or cornel wood about three feet long and a little thicker than a man's thumb, the sticks serving both for attack and for defence. I often fought thus, and in the end became one of the most expert; the net was work, but this was play. And personally I count it the most valuable kind of fencing, for one may often be caught in a fracas without arms, when if expert

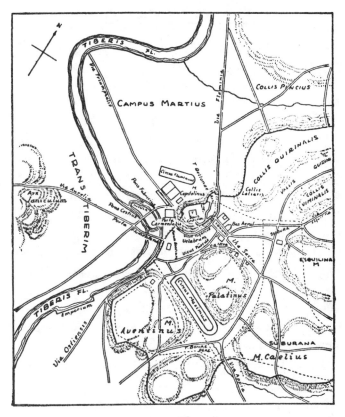

ROME IN CICERO'S TIME

with the cudgel he can make a stick or his belt-dagger serve as both sword and shield.

The other characteristic which all shared was their intense loyalty to certain ideals. Slaves though they were, and brutal in the extreme, they one and all were incredibly loyal to their master and to their code of honor. This code was a simple one, but had something of nobility in it; to die rather than strike a foul blow, and to do one's utmost for the school. So strong was this feeling, not only in our school but in others also, that I have known a gladiator, mortally wounded to send and ask his master if he had done enough; if so, he would be glad to lay down his arms and rest in death. And once, when one of our men was unfairly slain by a gladiator of the school of Norbanus, the victor's own mates slew him on his return to the barracks.

I cared for but few of the men in our school—or, for that matter, in any other—finding them for the most part dull-witted, ferocious, and unendurable; and having had but little education, I avoided my mates and tried as best I could to repair this lack of schooling. Being a slave, I could not earn money in my own right, but persons who had won through betting on our fights not infrequently gave the victor some small portion of their winnings, and Dumnorix allowed us to keep half of these gifts. Though most of the gladiators spent such presents on clothing, wine, or elaborately decorated armor, or gambled them away over the *tesserae* * or the *duodecim scripta,*† I used mine chiefly to purchase books, at first sending a slave to buy them, and later —when Dumnorix had come to trust me—going myself to the booksellers' shops in the Argiletum, and there browsing over the treasured rolls. The books were not expensive, as prices go; one could buy excellent copies for from one to ten *denarii,* and I found much pleasure in reading the poems of Homer, the tragedies of Aeschylus and Euripides (in translations, of course) and the comedies of Plautus, as well as some philosophy, so that in the course of my two years with the *lanista* I gained at least the rudiments of an education.

I did, however, strike up a friendship with a youth named Pugnax, and—so strangely do the Fates work in the affairs of men!—it was to this friendship that most of my later adventures were due.

Pugnax was a young man of my own age, from Gallia Transalpina—an Aeduan, to be exact—and he fought as a Samnite, with shield, helmet, and short sword. He was a rather homely, yellow-haired, merry, light-hearted youth, and a favorite with the crowds at Pompeii, Ravenna, and Baiae,

---

* Dice, exactly like our modern ones.
† A game of mingled chance and skill, somewhat resembling backgammon.

as well as at Rome, for the gay and sprightly manner of his fighting. His room-mate was slain in a bout a year or so after I came to the school, and since Murena had a friend who was alone, I asked and received permission to change my quarters and join Pugnax. Thereafter, we became great intimates, loving each other, and teasing each other continually. One of his favorite jokes was to declare that I must have Gallic blood in me.

"No true Latin ever wore such a flaming mop of hair, Tiberius," he would say. "Red as a game-cock's plumage! Your mother was a slave from Gaul, who escaped and married a Cilician pirate."

"Nay," I would answer, pretending wrath. "Never has one of my race worn the *braccae*." (For the Gallic men wear breeches instead of the Roman tunic.) "I may be a slave, but I come of the conquering race. In proof of which—" And then we would go into a friendly battle of fists.

For a long time we managed to avoid being matched against each other in the arena, the more readily since I believe Dumnorix had a secret liking for us both, and would have been sorry to have either slay the other. But in the end we were forced to fight, the manner of it being thus:

It was no uncommon thing for the more sporting members of the senatorial and equestrian orders to visit the schools, to inspect the gladiators and make up their minds how to bet on the coming fights. Frequent among such visitors was one Lucius Sergius Catilina, a man of about forty-five years, tall, handsome, muscular, active, and of great personal charm. It was said of him that he could bring to his way of thinking almost anyone with whom he talked, nor do I find this difficult to believe. It was said also that he was frightfully dissolute—in which respect, if true, he differed not at all from ninety-nine out of a hundred patricians—and even graver crimes were imputed to him. I believe, though, that these latter tales were invented by political enemies, to cast discredit on his name. I was quite a favorite of Catilina's, he having from time to time won considerable sums through betting on me, and he often presented me with a share of his winnings. A number of his friends generally came with him, but for these I did not care so much. There was one Publius Lentulus Sura, a self-satisfied, slow-witted mountain of fat, who had been consul, though certainly he must have used bribery to win the election; Gaius Cethegus, who though of good family and senatorial rank could outdo any of Dumnorix' men in coarse brutality; Quintus Curius—he was not so bad, though inclined to boasting; Titus Volturcius, whom I always suspected of being a coward, later events proving my estimate correct; Quintus Coeparius, a rat-faced libertine; and Publius Gabinius Capito, whose cognomen did not belie him, for his head was swollen with pride. The only ones I could like at all—save Catilina—were Lucius Vargunteius and Gaius Cornelius; they were courteous of manner, and possessed an alert, courageous look far different from the fat stupidity of Lentulus Sura or the savagery of Cethegus. Lentulus Sura, by the way, was the praetor whom I had seen at the auction when I was sold. Of the others, most were what Rome calls *"homo bellus"*—"pretty man." Sons of good families, they gave no thought to study or office or honorable employment, but only to the pursuit of pleasure. Bathed and oiled and bejeweled within an inch of their lives, their bare arms denuded of all hair and whitened like a woman's, their tunics and togas of purest wool whitened with fuller's earth, they spent their time in drinking, gambling, singing love songs, visiting the patrician ladies —anything to furnish amusement to their idle lives. I had no great respect for such as these; even the brutal Dumnorix seemed a more admirable figure.

It was not the custom of Dumnorix to match two men of his own school when it could be avoided, for in such case, whichever won, the master was sure to lose. But he could not always help doing so, and in May of my second year with him he matched me with Murena in certain games held at Ravenna. The expected result happened, and when we re-

turned to Rome I was still downcast; not that I
was particularly fond of Murena, but he was not a
bad sort, and I regretted his death. Having no
fondness for the butcher's trade, I had refused to
despatch him after bringing him down, whereat the
populace jeered and hooted me, and a dagger-man
finished the task. I may say here that it was this
trait of soft-heartedness which kept me from ever
becoming a favorite with the crowds, and I took
many a scourging before Dumnorix was finally convinced that in this respect he could not bend me to
his will.

The day after our return to Rome, Catilina, with
some friends, came to our barrack, and noting my
despondent air he asked the cause.

"Per Martes!" swore Dumnorix, "It is a weakness of the lad's. He has conquered Murena, has
seen him dragged out through the Porta Libitinensis, and he grieves like some girl mourning her pet
quail. What business has a gladiator with friends?"

"Or feelings?" broke in Vertumnus, a burly
Thracian whom I specially disliked. Then, contemptuously: *"Edepol!* He is a fool, this Tiberius!"

This angered me; in my young days my temper
was apt to be short.

"You lack the wit, Vertumnus," I snarled, "to
regret anything. A wolf has more bowels of compassion than you. And in truth, you are lower than

the beasts; they at least have the wit not to fuddle themselves with wine."

My reply touched him nearly. he having just been released from the stocks, where he had sat for drunkenness. He spluttered and swore, then as the visitors and some of the gladiators, pressing close, laughed at him, he leaped forward and struck at me with his fists. But a *retiarius* must needs be quick of motion, and I easily avoided the blow, planting my own fists in his stomach and knocking the breath from him. The crowd laughed more than ever, and he, recovering, gasped:

"Your life for that!"

"If you can take it," I jeered, and he turned to Dumnorix.

"Match me with him, *Domine*," he cried. "I will cut his comb, so hear me Pluto!"

"*Vae tibi!*" snorted Dumnorix, brushing him scornfully aside. "He would spit you as easily as old Coquus does a chicken! I have but one *secutor* fit to match with Tiberius."

"And who is that?" inquired Statilius, one of the visitors.

Dumnorix jerked his thumb toward my roommate.

"Pugnax, here," he answered. "They would make a good bout. I would bet even money on it."

Statilius raised his eyebrows.

"Even money, eh? And you intend to match them?"

Dumnorix laughed shortly.

"And lose one of my best men? Either of them is worth fifty *sestertia*."

"I would gladly pay well to see that bout," interjected Coeparius, and I think there was some malice in his suggestion, for it was well known that Pugnax and I were friends. "Eh, Gaius?" he went on, turning to Cethegus, who nodded, smiling a tight-lipped smile. "Why not make up a purse among us, to the value Dumnorix says, for the match? I will give ten *sestertia*."

"*Domine!*" I interrupted, horror-struck. "In the name of Mercury, do not do this! Pugnax is my best friend—my only friend! I beg of you!"

"Be silent!" the *lanista* ordered. "Who gave you leave to speak?"

"But—"

He silenced me with a blow that sent me sprawling; Dumnorix ruled us with no light hand.

Meanwhile the purse was being made up, only Catilina refusing to contribute.

"I will not pay to see friend slay friend," he told Coeparius.

In spite of Pugnax' protests and mine, the match was made, it being arranged that we were to fight at the games being given the following week by the aedile Piso, who was laying his plans for the consulship two years later, and was spending money with a free hand. I left the gathering, who were laying bets on the outcome, and went to my room, where I sat down on the edge of my bed, elbows on knees and head in my hands. Presently in came Pugnax, who seeing me thus in despair sat down beside me and flung his arm over my shoulders.

"Do not take it so hard, my Tiberius," he said. *"Mehercle!* what is a gladiator for but to die in the arena? Should you slay me, I promise to bear no ill will. And can you not find it in your heart to forgive me, the case being reversed?"

"Per Deos Immortales!" I cried, sitting up and flinging out my hands. "Do you think I fear death? Not so, Jupiter see me! But how can I fight you?" I jumped to my feet. "I will go to Dumnorix and tell him I refuse!"

He caught my tunic and dragged me back.

"Hear reason, Tiberius. What will that gain us? We shall simply be driven into the arena with red-hot bars and prodded therewith until we fight."

"Let them! I would rather be burned than fight you!"

"Verily! But how of me? They will be plying bar and whip on me also."

"Then I will let you slay me."

"That I may live with that memory? Nay, be

44

sensible, my Tiberius. This is our trade, and we have each confronted death too often to dread its face. And how of our honor? Is that not dear to you? It is to me. Come, come, my friend, we will give them a good fight, and whichever of us dies, he will go out with the plaudits of the crowd in his ears. Eh, my Tiberius?" And he hugged me again.

I was forced to admit the soundness of his reasoning; there was no escape from our fate. But the ensuing week was no pleasant one, nor when the appointed day came did I enjoy the march to the arena. This was a huge temporary wooden structure in the Campus Martius, open to the sky, and with benches rising tier above tier to its highest limits. No awnings had been spread, the senatorial and equestrian orders being seated on the shady side, and as we entered for our customary parade the building was jammed with at least forty thou sand spectators, a full third of them being women. The senators and Vestals sat in the front rows, flanking the box reserved for the *editor*, the giver of the games, and behind them were some five or six rows of knights, the remainder of the tiers being occupied by the people. This vast sea of faces, this buzz of talk, were of course no novelty to me, but on this day I felt well up within me a surge of bitter hatred for the heartless mob that had gathered to see me slay my friend; oddly enough, it never once occurred to me that Pugnax might be the victor.

According to custom, we paraded two by two, full-armed, about the arena, shouting our salute of *"Morituri te salutant!"* to the giver of the games, and as we did so I noticed that Piso was not occupying the *editor's* box. I nudged Pugnax, marching at my elbow.

"Who is that in the aedile's place?" I asked, and Pugnax chuckled.

"Cicero, the consul," he told me. "None other than Marcus Tullius himself. I hear that Piso is in bed with the gout, and has asked Cicero to take his place. Evil fortune for Piso, is it not, that he cannot show himself at his own games, and enjoy the gratitude of the people?"

But I was not interested in Piso's gout, and the parade being ended, I retired in gloomy silence to the guard-room, there to await my turn in the arena.

There were some two hundred pairs of gladiators, and since Pugnax and I were accounted among the best, we were reserved for the end, so had some time to wait. Of course, several pairs went on at a time, but even so it was a good three hours ere our names were called. As we rose to go out Pugnax stopped and held out his hand, which I grasped.

"No ill feeling?" he inquired.

"By all the Gods—" I choked, and could say no more.

The Gladiators' Barrack

I blinked as we stepped from the dusk of the
guard-room into the blaze of the arena, where the
afternoon sun was reflected upward from the white
sand, but by the time we had reached the *editor's*
box my eyes were adjusted and I could see perfectly
the grave yet kindly face of the consul looking down
at us. Not far from him sat Catilina, and I thought
I recognized on his features a look of sympathy
that was not to be found on those of the brutal
Cethegus or the malicious Coeparius. Saluting the
consul and each other, Pugnax and I fell to work.

For some time we dodged and feinted, I retreating, he always pursuing, dancing from side to side,
and ever changing the length of his stride as he did
so, while I watched for a chance to cast my net. At
length I made a cast, but my usual skill was lacking,
so that he avoided it cleverly and rushed at me, I
barely saving myself by taking to my heels. Heavy-
armored, he could not catch me, and I gathered my
net as I ran, then turned to face him. Again and
again this was repeated, and now we began to warm
up to it; I had forgotten, in the excitement of battle,
that it was my friend I was fighting. Gradually I
came to realize that we two were alone on the sand;
all the other bouts had ended, and all eyes were
focussed on us, who were giving the final exhibition
of the day. It may be that in glancing about I grew
careless; at all events, my foot slipped and I rolled

47

on the sand, feeling at the same time a stinging pain across my shoulders. I did not need the roar of the crowd to tell me that Pugnax' blade had raked my back, but I quickly rolled over twice and got to my feet before he could strike again; the wound was not deep, and I faced him with undimmed ardor, in my ears the shouts that greet a good fight.

Success so close, however, made Pugnax reckless, and as he rushed to follow up his advantage I cast my net, fairly entangling him in the folds. He was helpless, and instinctively I thrust with my trident, striking his thigh below the edge of his shield; he stumbled, dropped on one knee, and pitched forward, while a tremendous shout beat upward to the sky.

"*Habet!* Pugnax *habet!*" roared the crowd, mad with excitement. And again, "Pugnax *habet!*"

And with that I realized what I had done. My friend, my only friend, lay on the sand at my feet, his life at the mercy of that cruel mob that knows no mercy. And despair seized me in its grip; I felt a cold hand laid on my heart, the warmth of the sun drained away, and an icy chill shook me from head to foot.

I looked about that great arena, but saw no kerchief waved, no thumb down-turned in sign of pity; each arm was extended, each thumb, pointing to its owner's breast, said plainly, "Stab him!" I glanced toward the Vestals, but they sat silent and unmoved; it was beneath their dignity to notice so base a thing as a gladiator, and I was near the sacrilege of cursing them in my heart, even as I cursed that ferocious mob. Pugnax grinned up at me, saying:

"Do your duty, my Tiberius. No ill feeling!"

Stubbornly I planted my trident point down in the sand, then drew my dagger and planted that upright beside the trident, while a howl of rage and execration went up from all the benches. I saw the fatal Porta Libitinensis open, and from it issued slaves with ropes. No hope remained—yes, one; a vain one, I knew, but still a hope.

Stepping before the *editor's* box, I raised one finger in the gesture a defeated gladiator uses when asking mercy. For a moment my heart stood still, and then to my unspeakable delight Cicero drew from the bosom of his toga a kerchief and waved it twice!

And I am not ashamed to say that I was half blinded by tears of joy and gratitude as I lifted Pugnax in my arms and bore him from the arena.

CHAPTER III

Of the Thieves of the Subura; and the Meetings at Marcus Laeca's

ONE day about a week after my victory over Pugnax, we two were resting, he sitting on his cot and polishing his shield, while I stretched full length on my bed, reading aloud from the *Miles Gloriosus,* when Glaucus came to the open door and growled:

"Tiberius, you are wanted in the offices."

Reluctantly I laid aside the scroll, rose, and proceeded to the large room near the gate, where Dumnorix was wont to transact his business. There I found the *lanista* standing respectfully before a chair in which Catilina reclined, and as I entered he spoke abruptly to me.

"Tiberius, this gentleman wishes to purchase you, and I have agreed to let you go. As soon as the papers are drawn up, you are his."

"Not so fast," interrupted Catilina, smiling. "Let us first see whether or not I can depend on him for loyal service. Tiberius, have you an especial fondness for your present work?"

I thought of what I had been through during the

past two years, of the savage men among whom I lived, and of the hateful tasks of the arena.

"No, *Domine*," I replied. "Far from it."

"I want a good cudgel-player to give me my daily exercise, and Dumnorix tells me that you are his best. Also, I want a captain for my bodyguard. Do you think you could serve me faithfully?"

Apart from the joy of being freed from the arena, I was pleased at the thought of serving this man; I have already said that he was attractive. Something of my pleasure must have shown in my face as I answered, "Yes, *Domine*," for Catilina smiled.

"You may prepare the papers, Dumnorix," he said, and the *lanista*, bowing, went in search of his clerk, for he himself could neither read nor write.

When we were alone, Catilina regarded me thoughtfully for a moment, then asked:

"Tiberius, are you loyal to Rome? Is the welfare of the State dear to your heart?"

I thought this over; it seemed to me that I ought to answer yes, but for the life of me I could not. I shrugged my shoulders.

"What has Rome ever done for me save take me from the place where I was happy and force me to a loathsome task? No, *Domine*, I cannot truly say that I love Rome." It seemed to me that a flicker of satisfaction showed on his features, and I added, "Why do you ask?"

But before he could answer, Dumnorix returned with the papers, and Catilina, rising, asked the formal question of sale:

"Wilt thou give?"

"It shall be given," replied Dumnorix, and the two joined hands, the patrician then counting out fifty *sestertia*. After saying farewell and after receiving the thanks of the *lanista*, Catilina turned to go, but I stopped him.

"*Domine,*" I said, "I have but one regret in leaving this place."

He was quick of comprehension.

"Your friend Pugnax?"

"Exactly. Would you not buy him too, that we may be together?"

"It is more than I planned to spend," he reflected. "More, indeed, than I can afford. Still . . . Quintus Curius tells me that a friend of his, one Fulvia, also desires a captain of bodyguard. . . . I might buy Pugnax for him to give to her. . . . Well. . . ."

It was not quite what I had hoped for, but it was something to get Pugnax out of that place on any terms, and I thanked him. After some chaffering with Dumnorix, the second bargain was struck, and the three of us set off—Pugnax still limping a trifle from his wound—for my new master's home.

The greater part of Rome's business eddies and

THE ATRIUM OF CATILINE'S HOME

swirls about the Forum, and Catilina's home on the Palatine, not far from the Via Nova, was sufficiently removed to be out of the bustle, yet not so remote as to be difficult of access. It was not so extensive as many of the neighboring palaces, but plenty large enough for comfort, and it had evidently been a fine building, the walls and floors being faced with marble and adorned with exquisite mosaics, and the *atrium* containing a number of beautiful statues by Grecian sculptors. But of late years it had been allowed to run down as Catilina's circumstances were narrowed through dissipation—like nearly all patricians, he gambled heavily—or through unlucky investments in the East. This loss of money was amply proclaimed by the fact that the master's farm, together with all its slaves, had been sold to satisfy debts, and that the *familia urbana* was reduced to a mere forty slaves—an unusually small number for a Roman of the senatorial order.

Of these forty, ten were the bodyguard, an extremely competent set of fighters, hardy and well drilled, as I learned on my first inspection. My predecessor had recently died of the spotted fever, which accounts for my purchase, but since I had the disease in youth I did not fear to sleep in his room or to use his armor. This last was of a sort to delight the heart of any lover of good arms, being of the finest steel, ornamented with gold, and the shirt of mail being so fine and light that I could almost enclose it with my two hands, yet strong enough, as I afterward proved, to turn a sword-stroke. I was proud indeed when I donned this outfit and went to review my men among the columns of the *peristylium!*

I had no trouble with my ten rascals, who greeted me with respect: it seems that my reputation from the arena had gone before me, and as the unwounded victor in forty-two battles I commanded their admiration; this much good, at least, came from my servitude to Dumnorix. Having learned the names of my men and put them through their paces, I reported to Catilina, who acknowledged my report, then instructed me in my various duties, these being to drill my men, to accompany my master about the City, and to engage in a daily cudgel-bout with him. In these bouts we wore helmets and armor of leather, which made the fighting seem rather tame to me, but I could understand that it would not do for him to appear in public wearing bruises and cuts; after all, even the leather could not entirely prevent some such wounds.

We fenced daily for an hour or more, Catilina proving himself an excellent swordsman; he could have beaten any of Dumnorix' men save only myself, and even I had no more than a hair the better of him. At length, a week or so after my purchase, as we were resting from a bout, he said:

"Hold yourself in readiness to go with me this evening, Tiberius."

"Yes, *Domine,*" I responded. "I will notify the men."

"No," he contradicted. "Just you and I. We go to the house of a friend of mine, one Marcus Laeca, who lives in the Street of the Scythe-Makers. You know it?"

"In the Subura? Yes, truly. But with deference, *Domine,* that is a bad neighborhood. We would do well to take the guard."

"They would embarrass me. You will of course wear armor under your tunic, and carry a dagger."

"No sword?"

"No sword. I wish to appear a wholly peaceful citizen. We will start about the fourteenth hour. Do you rest this afternoon, for we may be late returning."

"Very well, *Domine.*" And bowing, I retired.

I did not like the prospect, and would vastly rather have taken the guard, for the Subura is by long odds the worst district in the entire City. It is the home of thieves, highwaymen, and professional assassins, all of whom find a safe retreat in its narrow and winding lanes and its hundreds of rickety tenements with their infinitude of doorways, boltholes, and alleys, so that the whole section is more like the labyrinth of Minos than any human dwelling-place. I marvelled that Catilina should have a friend in such a district, but I found later that Laeca's family had built there before the section ran down, and that he still clung to the home of his ancestors.

Catilina and I set out according to plan, I preceding him by a couple of paces and carrying a torch to light our steps, for by now the streets were dark. There was a moon, to be sure, which gave enough illumination in an open space like the Forum, but its rays could scarcely penetrate into the narrow ravines of the Suburan lanes. We met numbers of people in the Via Nova and as we crossed the Via Sacra, but they were mostly revelers—wealthy young patricians returning from late dinners or drinking bouts, rioting along with laughter and shout and song—and as we left the Forum and entered the Subura, passers-by were fewer. Those whom we did meet gave us a wide berth, not liking to go too near to strangers, until just as we turned into the Street of the Scythe-Makers there occurred precisely what I had feared—a rush of thieves from the mouth of a pitch-black alley.

The first warning I had was a patter of feet on my right, and I swung about to find myself confronting five desperate ruffians whose daggers gleamed in th.

torch-light. Three of them came at me, the other
two falling upon Catilina, and instinctively I dashed
my torch into the face of the foremost, so that he
reeled back, blinded and screaming; the pitch clung
to his skin and burned there. By now my dagger
was in my hand, and I stepped one pace to the right,
driving the steel up under the ribs of the next at-
tacker, who was not expecting a left-handed blow.
It finished him, but the third had some measure of
skill, and we fenced for perhaps a minute before I
got past his guard and was free to help my master.
Turning, I saw one of Catilina's assailants writhing
in the street, but the other, a huge man, had over-
thrown my master and, dagger lifted, knelt on his
arms. The robber's hand was descending in the
fatal blow as I caught his wrist and drove my dagger home under his left shoulder-blade. He gave a
convulsive start, stiffened, and rolled over, and I
assisted Catilina to rise.

"Neatly done, Tiberius," he commended, quite
cool and unperturbed. "This cursed toga hampers
a man. I envy you, who can go abroad in a tunic."

"The toga has its advantages," I reminded him
dryly. "Are you wounded?"

"In that it is the mark of a free-born citizen?
True, true. No, I am unhurt. And you?"

"Unhurt, *Domine*," I assured him.

"Then let us be on our way." He was arranging

his garments, and shrugged indifferently when I asked:

"What shall we do with these?" Indicating our late assailants; the first one, whom I had burned, had taken himself off.

"Leave them there," he said. "The scavengers will find them in the morning. . . . After all, Tiberius, it is by no means impossible that you may win your freedom; others have done so—many of them."

"Even then, I can never wear the toga."

He did not reply at once, but in a moment said, thoughtfully:

"I am by no means sure. If things go well. . . . However, let us proceed."

We were no more than a hundred paces from Laeca's door, which we reached at the same time as did a guarded litter. In the chief of the guard I recognized Pugnax, who greeted me with a cheerful grin as Quintus Curius, walking beside the litter, drew back the curtains. The occupant dismounted, and I saw that she was Fulvia, the woman who had bid on me against Dumnorix. She spoke pleasantly to Catilina, then to my surprise turned to me.

"Ha, Red-head!" she exclaimed. "How goes it? Well, I trust?" My face must have indicated surprise, for she laughed. "Oh, I have often watched that red thatch of yours in the arena since the day when Dumnorix and I had our battle of the *sestertia*.

And I have you to thank, indirectly, for my new chief guard. Well, the Fates be kind to you!"

"Thank you, *Domina,*" I answered, bowing, whereupon she smiled and passed with Curius and Pugnax into the house, Catilina following and signing to me to come also.

Within, we found Laeca, Lentulus Sura, Coeparius, Statilius, Vargunteius, and Cethegus; and a number of others whom I did not know. Lentulus Sura, Coeparius, and Laeca were whispering in one corner of the *atrium,* and they immediately drew Catilina into their discussion, while Curius and Fulvia joined the rest to watch Vargunteius and Cethegus at a game of *duodecim scripta.* Cethegus was losing, his coarse and brutal face flushed with rage because his opponent and the onlookers laughed at him, and the angrier he got, the more they laughed. Pugnax and I made ourselves unobtrusive in a corner, as became our station. Presently Cornelius arrived, and with him two whom I did not know; these three, together with Vargunteius and Curius, wore the *lacerna,* a short cloak which was much affected by fops in place of the toga.

"*Edepol!*" said Catilina to the newcomers. "I must adopt your style of dress. My toga went nigh to costing me my life this evening."

The company demanding particulars, he recounted our adventure, giving me full credit; and approving comments were addressed to me, compliments which I received with proper modesty.

"I would strongly advise you to wear the *lacerna*," remarked Lentulus Sura. "It has a further advantage for one in your position."

"And that?"

Lentulus gave a fat and silly snigger.

"The hood may be drawn over the face to form a disguise."

"Be silent!" snapped Laeca.

"Lentulus was always a fool," growled Cethegus, who by now was in an evil mood. "He always did talk too much."

I could hardly blame Lentulus for resenting this.

"Is that the way to speak to a praetor, an ex-consul?" he demanded, flaring up. "Cethegus, you are too free with your epithets."

Cethegus bounced to his feet.

"Would you care to teach me manners?" he demanded, thrusting his face close to Lentulus'.

Lentulus was no coward.

"Any time," he snapped, rising to meet the other.

The company flung themselves between the quarrelers, separating them and speaking soothing words.

"Not before the slaves," begged Laeca, motioning to Pugnax and me. Cethegus glanced at us.

"They can be—"

"Enough!" spoke up Catilina, the snap of authority in his voice. "Cethegus and Lentulus, sit down. Tiberius"—he turned to me—"do you and Pugnax stand guard outside the door, admitting no one whatever—"

"Sempronia is still to come," Vargunteius reminded him.

"Except Sempronia," Catilina amended. "You know her?"

"I do, *Domine,*" said Pugnax.

"Very well. To your posts."

Pugnax and I withdrew, Sempronia's litter being set down at the door just as we gained the street. She spoke to us pleasantly, in a peculiarly mellow voice which, however, had nothing in it of weakness, and she was at once admitted. As the door closed behind her Pugnax spat contemptuously on the pavement.

"What do you think of her, my Tiberius?" he asked.

"She is very beautiful," I replied. "And has a courtly manner. She spoke most graciously to us."

"Oh, she is charming enough, the Gods know well," he agreed. "And accomplished, also. She sings and dances marvellously, is educated far beyond the average, and has ten times the force of Fulvia. But—*Mehercle,* they two should be wearing the toga; the stola is for women of honor."

"Is she . . . are they. . . ."

Pugnax grinned.

"I see you are not acquainted with the gossip of the City, Tiberius. Did you not notice the pearls Sempronia wore? And the amber ball she carried to cool her palms. A thousand *sestertia* on her neck and arms—yet Decimus Brutus, her husband, is a poor man!"

I shrugged.

"I have but little inclination," I told him, "for scandal. What Fulvia and Sempronia may do is no concern of mine. Let them look to their actions; I to my own. What do you make of the affair within?"

"What do you mean?"

"It is too late for a dinner-party," I answered, thoughtfully. "And there are too many there—more than the couches would hold. I counted sixteen."

He drew nearer.

"Explain!" he said.

"I have been told," I went on, "that my master was implicated in a conspiracy a year ago, about the time Cicero and Antonius were elected consuls, and that it was frustrated. May this not be—"

"Another such?" Pugnax laughed and slapped me on the back. *"Per Martes,* you are not so stupid after all, my Tiberius! But it is not well

63

for slaves to know too much; these patricians are even more liberal with yoke and lash than our old friend Dumnorix, and a deaf ear may well save us a scarred back."

But my curiosity had been aroused.

"I am going to see if there is not some way to listen."

He caught my arm.

"You fool! Do you desire the cross? Would you be thrown, living, to the eels in Laeca's fishpond, for them to tear the flesh from your bones? Have sense, Tiberius!"

"Pooh!" I answered. "The worst I have to fear is a whipping, and that is no novelty to us. I am too valuable to be slain. Would Catilina throw fifty *sestertia* to Laeca's eels?"

Pugnax still tried to dissuade me, but my mind was fixed and I went looking for a way to mount the roof; I had an idea.

Laeca's house, one story in height, stood on a corner, and some way down the side street was a low wine-shop, from which came the words of a ribald song shouted by drunken men. Counting on this to cover any trifling noise I might make, I slipped off my corselet and scandals, then bade Pugnax lean over and give me a back. He lamented the fate I was about to bring down on both our heads, but did as I wanted, and mounting on his shoulders I sprang and caught the edge of the roof. By main strength I drew myself up, got on the tiles, and tip-toed across them until I reached the edge of the *impluvium*.* By good fortune the company were in the *atrium* beneath, and through the opening I could hear what was said as plainly as though I were in the room with them.

It was soon clear to me that I was right; a conspiracy was on foot, my master being the leading spirit. I heard a long discussion of ways and means, of who should do thus and so, and of various dates for the breaking out of the revolt; and I gathered that it was to be a general rebellion. The conspirators were planning to take the City, to establish Catilina as consul, to distribute the various offices among the band, to loot the Treasury, to proscribe many leading citizens to death—in short, to overthrow the government and seize the power exactly as Lucius Cornelius Sulla had done twenty years before. As I now look back on that night of three decades gone, I suppose I should have been shocked at what I heard—indeed, had my station

* The roof of a Roman house sloped toward a rectangular opening over the center of the *atrium,* or main room. This opening, the *impluvium* ("place for the rain to come in") admitted light and air as well as rain, the water dripping into a basin whose edge was flush with the floor, and being led thence into cisterns. The words *impluvium* and *compluvium* are used indifferently by Roman writers to designate both the opening in the roof and the basin beneath.

in life been what it now is, I would have been. But then the youthful blood ran hot in my veins, I was eager for adventure, had the young man's indifference to responsibility, and all in all I was interested rather than outraged. I held my place on the roof until the meeting showed signs of breaking up, then I tip-toed back to the edge and dropped to the street. I had donned my sandals and was buckling on my corselet when I heard the street door open and Catilina's voice ask sharply:

"Where is Tiberius?"

Per Martes, I was fairly caught!

What to do? For though I had made light of Pugnax's words, I knew well enough that something worse than a mere whipping was in store for me; what I had heard told me that the conspirators were desperate men, to whom the life of a slave was less than that of a worm beneath the wheel, and the fate of one caught spying on them would be no enviable one. I had visions of myself spread-eagled on a cross; of being hurled, bound hand and foot, into Laeca's fish-pond; of the *lorarius* tearing my back to ribbons with his lash until I dropped and died under the torture. What to do? Dash for the City gates, pass them on some pretext, and try to reach the Sabine Hills, to join some band of outlaws? Small chance! Run to the consul and denounce the conspirators, throwing myself on his mercy? I would most likely be executed out of hand, along with any others who might be caught; or if I escaped that I would be the target for a hundred assassins' daggers. Or throw myself on the crowd, selling my life as dearly as possible ere going down under the weight of numbers? These thoughts flashed through my mind in an instant, and I had about decided on a rush for the gates when I heard Pugnax say:

"He was here but a moment since, *Domine*. He stepped down to the wine-shop for a drink. I am watching till he returns."

"Go fetch him," ordered Catilina, harshly.

"Yes, *Domine*."

I blessed Pugnax' quick wit; this meant no more than a whipping. And forthwith I marched boldly around the corner, wiping my mouth on the back of my hand.

Never do I hope to listen to such a tongue-lashing as my master gave me! They spoke truly who said he had the gift of words, for though he used no oaths, no foul language, and no abuse, within two minutes I felt myself the smallest thing ever made; at my own valuation, I could have donned a plumed helmet and walked upright through the crack under Laeca's door.

"And when I give an order I expect and will have instant, unquestioning, and complete obedience under pain of severest punishment," he told me. "I treat my slaves well when they do their duty, but am not moved by any foolish compassion when they disobey." Suddenly his voice grew mild. "But for what you did earlier in the evening, your back would know the lash. I cannot, though, give the word to punish one who has so lately saved my life. You are forgiven—this time."

"I thank you, *Domine*," I answered, humbly, and taking my torch I preceded him home.

The ensuing weeks taught me the truth of what Catilina said. I cannot imagine slaves being better treated than his were so long as they tried to do right, and he was always indulgent to honest ignorance or misunderstanding. But let one of the *familia* disobey wilfully, and the punishment meted out to him would set the others whispering for a week. On the whole, Catilina was a good master, never demanding impossibilities, never punishing unreasonably, and always quick to reward any special merit with words of commendation or with some trifling sign of favor—a cup of choice Falernian wine, a tidbit from the table, a small coin—and always the manner of giving was worth more than the gift itself. During the few months of my service with him I grew to be no little fond of Lucius Catilina.

Some two nights after the meeting. Pugnax and

I were again stationed at Laeca's door, and I took that opportunity of telling my friend what I had overheard. He thought the information over, then asked:

"What do you mean to do? Betray them?"

"Do? Nothing. Why should I betray them? What is to gain by doing so?"

"We might be given our freedom," he answered.

"We might, yes. But I ask you, is it likely?" And he was forced to admit that it was not. "On the other hand," I went on, "should the revolt succeed, it is more than probable that we shall win our desire. Cethegus is to call out the slaves in the City with that promise, and in any case there will be fine looting."

Pugnax nodded.

"There is, however," he mused, "the small matter of loyalty to the State."

"Edepol! Be reasonable, Pugnax. What loyalty do you or I owe to Rome? What has Rome done for us, save snatch you from your home in Gallia Transalpina and me from mine on the Mare Illyricum, and make slaves of us?"

"It was the pirates who stole you, not Rome," he offered.

"And why? Would they have done it had they not known there was a ready market for me in the City? No, Pugnax, Rome is to blame for that.

We owe the State as much allegiance as Spartacus owed—no more, no less."

"You may be right," he nodded. "Certainly there is reason in what you say. And certainly, too, I have sworn no allegiance."

"Further yet," I urged, "who is to say that Catilina's government will be worse than the present one? Now, the *optimates*—as they proudly call themselves—that is, the senatorial and equestrian orders, control the State, but do they rule it for the welfare of the people? A foolish question! I grant that Marcus Cato, Gaius Caesar, and perhaps a half-dozen others are honest men, but we know very well that the most of them use their power for themselves alone. Look what Verres did in Sicilia. Oh, I have been studying politics, my Pugnax! And the restoring of the tribuneship—was that for the welfare of the people? And Catilina has in his party a number of senators and knights—"

"Many of whom," Pugnax interrupted, "were expelled from office for misconduct."

"For misconduct? Or through jealousy? And is it likely that Catilina's men would be worse than those now in office?"

"The consul is a good man," he demurred.

"Which consul? Cicero, yes; I grant you that." I flung my arm around his shoulders. "I would be the last to speak a word against the man who gave me you. But Antonius? Bah! And the praetors and aediles?"

He laughed shortly.

"They are naught to boast of, it is true. Then it is your thought to let matters take their course?"

"Have you a better plan to suggest?"

He shook his head, saying:

"There is one thing, and only one, that makes me doubtful. In all this rioting and burning that are planned, no one's life will be safe. Now, you and I, being fighting-men, can take our chance, and likely come off with whole skins. But there is a girl at my mistress' home who is dear to me—I met her while we were still in Dumnorix' school, and have seen much of her since Curius gave me to Fulvia—and it would break my heart if aught should happen to her."

"If she is Fulvia's slave she will be safe enough," I answered. "In any case, you can doubtless protect her. And the more reason to seek your freedom and hers, for unless you are both free you cannot wed her honorably. You mean to wed her?"

He grasped my arm, speaking with unwonted earnestness.

"Tiberius, I thought I was hard within, but Venus hear me, I am pierced through and through with the golden arrow of Cupid. I would see all Rome in flames ere harm should come to one finger of my Polla—"

"*Who?*" I demanded. "Describe her!"

He stared at me in amazement.

"You know her?" he asked.

"How can I tell? Describe her."

He drew a long breath.

"She is the most exquisite creature!" he rhapsodized. "Small, slight-built, dainty, with hair like the raven's wing, eyes of richest brown, a small nose delicately turned, a mouth designed by Venus herself for man's allurement—"

"Return to earth, man! Do you think yourself Homer, singing the charms of Menelaus' bride? How old is she? How tall? Does she speak with a trifling lisp?"

"She does indeed! The most adorable lisp! For the rest, she is fifteen or sixteen, her head comes just to my shoulder, she is slim and graceful as Diana's self, with a profusion of blue-black curls, and she has a trick of catching her tongue between her teeth and dropping her head to look up from under her lashes—this when she is teasing. Do you know her? *Edepol!* And in the school we thought you a very anchorite. You rogue! Tiberius—" he was suddenly grave "—Tiberius, if you take her from me you and I shall fight, and not with net and trident."

"Be content," I told him. "She is my sister."

"Your sister!" He gaped at me.

"My foster-sister, that is. I have not seen her since the day we stood on the block in the Forum Boarium. Be content, my Pugnax; there is no man in all the City I would rather see her wed. But the more reason to seek our freedom."

"Per Deos Immortales, yes! Well, ho for the revolt! Let Cethegus but come to me with the word, and he shall find me ready."

Through July and August the meetings of the conspirators were held at Marcus Laeca's, but early in September I was responsible for their being transferred to Catilina's. Not intentionally—far otherwise!—but none the less it was my doing, the manner of the change being thus:

Pugnax and I continued to listen to the conferences, being, however, more careful not to be found out. That is, I listened while he kept guard, and through my eavesdropping I became thoroughly familiar with the plans of the conspirators. It was perhaps not altogether honorable of me to listen as I did, but I strongly desired my freedom, and a slave is not bound by the ties of honor that hedge a noble. And ere any condemns me, I would ask that he himself eat the bitter bread of slavery for two long years; should he then feel that I was to blame, I am willing to bear the censure.

At all events, I listened, and thus learned that the plan was for a double uprising. Gaius Manlius, a veteran centurion of Sulla's, was to gather and organize an army of the disaffected, holding it in readiness near Faesulae; Catilina, Cethegus, Lentulus Sura, Longinus, Laeca, Annius, and several others were to remain in the City, organizing the restless element there—the slaves, a part of the freedmen, and the unruly of the populace. And on an appointed date Manlius was to appear before Rome with his army, while those within were to fire the City in many places, to slaughter any citizens who opposed them, and thus create a terror and confusion during which the conspirators would open the gates to the army, seize the reins of government, name Catilina consul, and proscribe and loot such senators and knights as refused to join them.

Well, to return. One warm evening in September Pugnax and I were stationed as usual before the house in the Street of the Scythe-Makers, and according to custom I climbed the roof to listen. The day had been hot, so that the awning was drawn across the *impluvium,* and though it rained during the afternoon the lazy slave in charge had forgotten or neglected to withdraw the cloth. I do not understand why Laeca allowed it to remain in place through the evening, but it may be that absorption in the plot prevented his noticing it. At any rate, there it was, and tended to muffle the voices of those in the *atrium*. Crouching near the edge of the opening in order to hear, suddenly I was aware of a noise behind me, and as I turned quickly I saw someone creeping toward me down the sloping roof. At that moment the scudding clouds parted, and in the moon's full light I recognized one of Laeca's slaves, hands outstretched, intent on capturing me; whether he also came to spy on the conspirators or was protecting his master's house, I never knew. Instantly I realized that it was his life or mine; realized that should I slay him the wound would reveal my presence—or at least that of some person—on the roof; and further, that the slippery tiles, still wet from the rain, offered an excellent chance for two struggling men to fall together into the *atrium*. And I had a flash of amusement as I pictured the consternation of the plotters if we should tumble, heels over head, in each other's arms, into the midst of the conference.

But it was no laughing matter. I knew very well that it was death to me to be caught there, so as he grasped at me I ducked under his hands and with all my strength brought my fist up under his jaw. His head snapped back, his knees sagged, and as he tottered to fall I caught him about the waist, spun around, and hurled him through the *impluvium*. I heard the awning rip from its fastenings, heard the splash with which he landed in the basin beneath, and heard a startled oath and a woman's scream, but I did not wait; in truth, at that moment I was scrambling up the tiles to drop to the street, snatch up my arms, and rush around the corner.

I had barely taken my place when the door opened and Laeca thrust forth his head. Pugnax and I stiffened to attention; he glanced suspiciously from one to the other of us, and withdrew. The Gods be thanked, he did not notice that my sandals were unlaced!

"What has happened? Tell me!" demanded Pugnax, excited.

"Hush!" I answered, stooping to lace my footgear. "Did you hear anything?"

"*Per Martes!* I heard Sempronia scream."

"Naught else?"

"No."

"Stick to that if questioned. I will explain at some future time."

However, we were not examined. But next day I learned that Cethegus dragged the slave from the basin and despatched him before he could speak, thus precipitating a fine wrangle, for Laeca maintained quite properly that Cethegus had no right to execute justice on a slave without the owner's permission, and Vargunteius felt that the spy should have been questioned before being sent to join his ancestors.

This was almost the last of the Suburan meetings; the conspirators—not without reason—felt doubtful of Laeca's slaves. Two other meetings were held, later, in the Street of the Scythe-Makers, and I will tell of these in their proper place, but for a time the councils were transferred to Catilina's home, and this resulted in my being taken into the conspiracy.

The morning after my narrow escape, Catilina summoned me to his presence. The *vestiplicus* had just arranged his toga, and he was half sitting, half reclining—so as not to disarrange the folds—on a couch. He motioned me to draw near, then, speaking in a low voice:

"Tiberius, do you desire freedom?"

"What slave does not, *Domine?*" I answered, respectfully.

"And you would not be overly scrupulous as to the means whereby it came?"

"I do not understand you, *Domine*. Naturally, like all things, freedom can be bought too dear."

"Well . . . a bit of rioting . . . a trifle of an insurrection . . . street fighting . . . they would not shock you?"

I grinned.

"*Domine,* I was for two years a gladiator, and fought some forty times in the arena."

"Good! Then swear by the spirits of your

77

fathers and by Jupiter the All-Father that never by word or look will you reveal what I am about to tell you."

"I do so swear."

And with that he told me the entire plan of the conspiracy, as I had overheard it, together with some details that I did not know. At the conclusion:

"Are you with us, Tiberius?"

"Heart and soul, *Domine*. As I see it, the worst that can happen is death"—I touched the bronze hilt of my dagger to avert the evil omen—"and success means freedom and wealth. Who could hesitate?"

"Excellent!" said he. "Then to-morrow night, when our party meets here, do you stand guard on the roof to prevent spying." And he told me of the death of Laeca's slave.

"Pugnax will guard the door?" I inquired.

"As hitherto, yes."

"Then had I not better tell him of our plans? Otherwise he will wonder. And I know that he will feel as I do."

Catilina thought for a moment.

"Can you answer for his fidelity?"

"As for my own."

"H'm!" Then, reflectively: "A sound man is always good to have with us. . . . Well, go to Fulvia and ask if I may borrow her chief bodyguard for an hour this afternoon. Have him here at the seventh hour; I will forego my siesta for the day." And with a wave of his hand he dismissed me.

Pugnax took the oath and joined the plot as readily as I had done—why should he not?—and from that time on we were full-fledged conspirators, kept abreast of the plans without effort of our own.

CHAPTER IV

Of the Camp of Manlius; and the Extreme Decree

ONE morning about the Kalends of October,* Catilina sent for me.

"Tiberius," he began, "in one of the bed-chambers you will find a quantity of daggers and swords. Place these in my litter and to-night at midnight convey them to the home of Cethegus. You know where it is?"

"In the Via Sacra. Yes, *Domine*."

"Even so. Take my regular bearers—"

"With respect, *Domine,* I would not choose them."

"Why not?"

"They are not fools. I would take more stupid ones, as being less likely to think, and therefore less apt to talk."

"You at least are no fool," he smiled.

"The arena sharpens a man's wits, *Domine*."

"Doubtless it does. Well, then, as you say. At midnight Cethegus will expect you."

---

* October 1.

"With all deference," I remonstrated, "I would prefer midday to midnight."

"In the name of Mercury, why?"

"Observe, *Domine,* that the only persons abroad at midnight are of the Subura—thieves and the like —or else revelers of the patricians. Now, as you well know, midnight revelers do not take to their litters until so drunk they cannot walk. But all Rome knows that your vice is not wine but gambling—" I had won favor enough to dare speak thus freely "—and should your litter be seen at midnight folk would say 'What! Is Catilina drunk at last?' And it would arouse comment. On the other hand, should we go at midday there is but little chance of any seeing us, the streets being utterly deserted through the siesta hour. Indeed, so empty are they that I have read a ghost story whose author thought it proper to lay the scene in the Forum at midday."

He nodded.

"I know the tale. And there is much to your argument. To-morrow, then, when the shadows are shortest."

"These arms, *Domine*—they are for the revolt?"

"Naturally. For the slaves and freedmen within the City. Cethegus is gathering a store of weapons. And I have other stores at various points throughout Italia."

"I understand. To-morrow at noon." And receiving permission, I withdrew.

It was strange to see the Forum, usually so crowded and bustling with life, standing deserted under the blaze of the noon-day sun. At night one might fairly expect to find it empty, but now there was a weird and eerie quality about its emptiness, a feeling as though all life were suspended. The shops along both sides were vacant, the Argiletum was deserted, no one moved in the Via Nova or the Via Sacra, and not least strange was the fact that I could see for long distances. Ordinarily the eye is stopped in the foreground—or at most a few score paces off —by the thronging figures of men and women, but now great vistas opened before me, and I seemed to be walking in a world of spirits that pressed all about me, watching my every move, themselves invisible, soundless. And over all the hot blaze of the sun. It was most uncanny, the more so because all that broke the silence was the patter of our sandals on the pavement. The bearers felt it also, as I could tell by the nervous way in which they kept glancing about them, and I myself half expected to meet the ghost of whom I had spoken to Catilina. And so great was the tension that I jumped and the bearers almost dropped the litter when a pariah dog came lurching toward us around a corner.

But use accustoms us to all things, and before

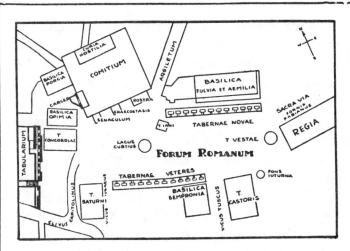

THE ROMAN FORUM IN CICERO'S TIME

many days were past we could make the trip unmoved by nervousness; indeed, I came to enjoy it, finding a pleasurable thrill in being abroad in a deserted city. For we made a number of such journeys; the conspirators were bringing in all the arms they could collect, and in the end we filled several rooms of Cethegus' house.

I was kept busy for some time at this work, and was therefore unable to carry out an idea which I had, but at length Fortuna brought about my wish. One afternoon when I returned from Cethegus', Catilina sent for me, placing his tablets in my hands.

"These letters to Quintus Curius at once," he said. "By your own hand. You will most likely find him at Fulvia's. And bring an answer."

Saluting, I went out, and curiosity inspired me to read the letter, but honor restrained me; since Catilina had of his own free will received me into the plot I could no longer plead curiosity, and it would be the act of a sneak to spy on him. In any case, I could not have opened the tablets, for the cord binding them was drawn tight. I did notice, however, that the seal was not Catilina's own signet, but some special device which he had newly adopted.

At Fulvia's I was told that Curius was not there, but was expected later, and I decided to wait for him. The *janitor,* an ill-conditioned brute, was for having me wait in the street, but for various reasons

The Extreme Decree

I declined to do so, and demanded that I be allowed to enter the house.

"Fulvia knows me," I told him. "Let me be taken before her, and see if she thrusts me from the door."

"My mistress sleeps," he answered. "Nor will I wake her from her siesta for any fly-by-night with pierced ears and scarred back. Be off, or I will call her chief of guard."

"Do so," I grinned. "By all means do so, half-wit. Nothing could give me greater pleasure."

Growling, he took me at my word, and sent a slave in haste for Pugnax, with the prompt result that I was invited in and the doorkeeper got a rating. Pugnax led me to the *peristylium*, where he seated me on a bench in the shade of a plane tree, and called for cool wine. When it was brought he whispered to the slave, who nodded and disappeared, while Pugnax and I sipped our wine and chatted. Presently two soft hands were slipped over my eyes from behind, and a well-remembered voice spoke in my ear:

"Who is it? Guess!"

"Polla!" I cried, and the next instant we were in each other's arms; we had not seen each other for two long years.

By and by, when questions had been asked and answered, Polla and Pugnax sat down on the bench, I taking a seat on the grass before them. Hand in hand they sat, while she told me of her life with Fulvia. This latter, it seemed, was no bad mistress; kind in the main, though subject to violent headaches and apt to be impatient when so afflicted. Being quick to learn and deft of hand, Polla had been made hair-dresser to her mistress, and led an easy life, with little to do, and many privileges. On the whole—and glad I was to hear it—my little sister was not unhappy, and was saving up her gifts and perquisites to buy her freedom; she calculated that in four years more she would be able to do so. At this I glanced at Pugnax, who shook his head slightly, whereby I knew that he had wisely kept secret the plans of our conspiracy.

We enjoyed a good hour of chat, then I was summoned within, finding Curius there, and to him I delivered the letter. He cut the cord, read the message, and sent for Pugnax. The latter being come, Curius said:

"Pugnax, Catilina desires to borrow you for a few days; you will report to him."

Returning to Catilina's, we learned what was wanted, for Pugnax was given a heavy bag of gold and an eagle such as is carried before a legion. But instead of being bronze, this one was of solid silver.

"These to Manlius at Faesulae, with all speed," said my master. "You will find a horse waiting for you at the Porta Tiburtina. Take the Via Tiburtina until well clear of the City, then strike west by cross-roads to the Via Aurelia, and so north. The gold is for Manlius to use as he sees fit; the eagle is to be his standard. And bid him not dishonor it, for it was my ancestor's and now is mine; it was carried by the legions of Gaius Marius against the Cimbri.

"Give him also this message, which I will not commit to writing. On the fourth day before the Kalends of November he is to put his army in motion, marching south, and on November's Kalends he is to take the stronghold of Praeneste. He will garrison it, and hold himself in readiness to descend on Rome. Understood?"

"Understood, *Domine.*"

"Repeat it."

Pugnax did so, and Catilina nodded approval, then dismissed him, and he set out.

A week or so passed uneventfully, then Pugnax returned and reported the success of his mission. I had a chance to talk with him, and found him no little disheartened.

"Manlius is a good leader," he told me. "An able leader, and experienced. As to weapons, tents, supplies—everything pertaining to a camp—he is in excellent shape, but it would require a year's time to beat discipline into that mob of his. Of all the riff-raff! It was sickening."

"They are worthless?"

"*Homines perditi*—lost men. Oh, they will fight; make no mistake about that! But they are the very scum of the earth. Some veterans of the army, but mostly gladiators, rebellious colonists of Sulla's, and the off-scouring of the country towns—thieves, broken men, assassins, and the like. The Gods pity Rome when that mob is turned loose within the walls! I will say this for Manlius, that he has refused to enlist runaway slaves, but for the rest—!"

"That is Catilina's policy," I told him. "My master fears that should he employ runaway slaves it would prejudice the City against him."

"Prejudice—! *Per Deos Immortales!* If that unholy collection of scoundrels does not prejudice Rome against him there is naught that can. Ten thousand of them—two full legions—and not one in ten but is ripe for the cross. Why, Tiberius, the Gods see me, I believe there are men there who, given the chance, will violate the Shrine and Hearth of Vesta! And he is calling out the slaves of the City; why not those of the farms?"

"You know well that the urban slaves are far less brutal and savage than the rustic ones."

"H'mph! As though aught could be worse than the crowd he has!"

"Well, we must use what weapons come to hand,"

I reminded him. "And we can hardly expect the aid of the wealthy citizens."

Pugnax laughed shortly.

"True enough, my Tiberius. Especially since they are the ones at whom we aim our daggers. Well, the Fates send us good fortune—though I shudder to think what we shall see when the gates lie open to Manlius."

Shortly after Pugnax' return—I remember it was the twelfth day before the Kalends of November * —I attended my master when he went to a meeting of the Senate. The previous day, a messenger from the consul had gone about, notifying the senators, and they met, as usual, in the Curia Hostilia, just off the Forum, to the north. Of course I did not enter the Senate chamber, but was stationed with other attendants just outside the door, so I could see and hear perfectly what went on within.

When all were seated, Cicero arose to address the assembly. He was a tall man, very thin, with the pallor of a student rather than the color of an out-door man, and his face was one of the homeliest I have ever seen. From slightly stooping shoulders there rose a long, thin neck like that of a crane, to support a high-domed, partly bald head with aquiline nose and dark brown eyes, which last, weakened by much study and reading, puckered slightly, and

* October 21.

now looked as though strained with anxiety. Indeed, his whole face had a worn and tired air, but when he began to speak I forgot all this, forgot his homeliness and lack of grace, and listened with all my ears. He was a *novus homo,* a "new man"; that is to say, one whose ancestors had held no curule office, but who by sheer genius had lifted himself to the highest office within the State, and as such he was somewhat looked down upon by those patricians whose homes could show hundreds of waxen masks of honored ancestors. But if he felt any inferiority no sign of such feeling was manifest in his voice, which was clear, assured, and the most musical I have ever heard. His choice of words, too, was marvellous, his sentences perfectly turned, and as his flexible tones flowed on, rising in indignation or sinking in appeal, I did not wonder that in a nation of orators he was esteemed the foremost, that when he spoke in public the Forum and the surrounding roofs were crowded with those who came to hear.

But if the manner of his speech charmed me, he had spoken no more than a few sentences when I was filled with horror, for he was telling the Senate the details of our conspiracy! His spies had served him well, for he seemed to know everything—of the army at Faesulae, the weapons at Cethegus', the meetings in the Street of the Scythe-Makers, the plan to call out the slaves of the City—everything.

"And, *Patres Conscripti*," he said, "if I name no names, it is not for lack of knowledge, but because I have as yet no legal proof. Let me but force the conspirators into the open, let me but gain the unquestionable evidence of their crime, and as the Gods look down upon us, you shall know them all!"

A sick despair filled my bosom as he ended, and I began to think of flight, to wonder in what little village of Etruria or Sabinum I could hide. But then, glancing through the doorway, I saw my master calm and unmoved, a faintly contemptuous smile playing upon his lips, and I was somewhat reassured; certainly this could not be so terrible a matter if Catilina was able to sit and smile.

A long and heated debate followed when Cicero sat down. Marcus Cato, known for his rigid and unbending honor, was for asking the consul the names of those implicated and placing them at once under arrest; he was never one to sacrifice honesty to expedience, and his unthinking morality was at times an embarrassment to his friends. Gaius Iulius Caesar, as was to be expected, spoke more temperately; the State, he said, was strong enough to protect itself; let them double the guards within the wall, send an army to encounter Manlius, and trust to the consuls to defend the lives and property of the citizens. The other consul, Antonius, spoke also, but said little, temporizing and repeating himself, saying that he feared his colleague was unduly alarmed, and that he himself could perceive no danger. I smiled inwardly at this, for I knew that he had been invited to join our conspiracy, and though he declined, naming his consular position for an excuse, he privately sent word to my master that he was in sympathy with us. Other speakers followed, and at length my master rose.

He had felt, said Catilina, the consul's eyes fixed accusingly on him, and he knew that, because he was implicated in an earlier plot, there would not be lacking those to hold suspicion of him now. But before all the Gods he would swear that he was innocent of any purposed treason against the State, and any who suspected him did so unjustly; he had entirely abandoned his designs on the consulship, and Rome now had no more loyal son than himself.

"And in proof of this," he concluded, "I will give myself into the custody of any magistrate whom the Senate may name, to be his prisoner until such time as this conspiracy is wholly cleared up and the guilty ones are known and punished."

Catilina spoke well, and his words had their effect, for when he sat down many of the senators cheered him. Cicero, to be sure, wore a sour smile which proved that he was not convinced, and Caesar's lips twitched with amusement, while Cato's face showed its usual grim disgust with a sordid world—strange that unbending virtue should make a man so unlovable!—but the greater part of the assembly was confident of my master's innocence. As for myself, I was utterly amazed at such unblushing effrontery, and in that moment I knew myself unfit to lead a conspiracy; Mercury himself, the father of trickery and craft, could never have enabled me to tell so plain, direct, and circumstantial a falsehood.

The debate continued long past the usual hour for rising, and when the senators at length adjourned for the night it was planned to meet again on the following day; nothing had been decided in that mighty ocean of words. Catilina retired early to slumber, saying naught to anyone of the day's events.

Next day the debate was resumed, and late in the afternoon two decisions were reached. First, that an army should be equipped, placed under command of the praetor Metellus Celer, and sent out to meet Gaius Manlius. Second, that the Senate should pass the Extreme Decree, used only in times of utmost peril, the decree which places absolute power in the hands of the consuls, enable them to enlist troops and order their movements, to arrest citizens—in fact, makes them for the time being dictators; the decree which runs: "Let the consuls see to it that the State takes no harm." And with this last, the meeting adjourned.

I was sent flying to the houses of all the conspirators, to summon them to a meeting that night at Catilina's, and about the fourteenth hour they began to assemble. It was plain from their looks and manner that the doings in the Senate had shaken them. Lentulus Sura's fat face was a-quiver with trepidation; Cethegus swore venomously under his breath in almost a continuous stream of oaths: and Coeparius, pale and terrified, kept glancing nervously about him as though he feared a *lictor's* hand upon his shoulder. Fulvia, all in a nervous twitter, could not keep her hands still, but played them flutteringly, now here, now there, about her garments and her jewelry. And all save two showed white and drawn of countenance. Those two were my master for one, and for the other, Sempronia, wife of Decimus Brutus. That night I was forced to grant Sempronia my reluctant admiration; dissolute she was, beyond all question, faithless to an honorable husband, and lost to all sense of virtue; but, *per Deos Immortales,* in a group of trembling cowards she displayed the unmoved courage of a Roman matron. And when any speaks against her, as many have done, I think of that night and say to myself: "Bad she may have been, but at least she was brave."

The Extreme Decree

The debate that night in Catilina's *atrium* was no
whit less acrimonious than the one which had taken
place in the Curia Hostilia—rather more so, in
fact. It was the first time I had been allowed to
stay in the room at one of our meetings, but when
I asked, "Shall I take my usual post, *Domine?*"
Catilina replied, "No. Remain here."

"Are you not going to have the *impluvium*
guarded?" asked Vargunteius, and Catilina cynically
answered:

"To what end? Cicero knows that we are con-
spiring, nor could any spy do us more harm than a
traitor has already done." He rose to his feet.
"And that is one task for to-night," he went on.
"To find and punish the one who has betrayed us."

"And how, forsooth, are we to do that?" Statilius
demanded.

"Has anyone any suspicions?" asked Catilina
looking about.

They glanced at one another doubtfully, and
finally Cethegus offered:

"Lentulus is a fool; he may have let his tongue
wag."

"Cethegus," burst out Lentulus, "if you say I am
a traitor, you lie!"

"I did not mean of set intent," Cethegus denied.
"But you are loose-mouthed, and may have blabbed
without knowing you did so."

"Intentionally or not—you lie!"

"More likely," interposed Curius, "that Coeparius has been overcome by fear and has run to the consul with the tale, under promise of immunity; he has no more courage than a hare."

"I did not, I swear I did not!" babbled the one accused, turning white to the lips. "By the Hearth of Vesta, I swear I am as loyal as any here!"

"What of Laeca's slaves?" inquired Statilius. "Might they not have listened?"

Catilina turned this over in his mind, then finally negatived the idea.

"Cicero knows of things," he explained, "that have been decided since we have been meeting here."

"How of your own?" Statilius persisted. "How of Tiberius, here?"

"I will be answerable for his fidelity," my master assured them.

"Still," Cethegus suggested, "it might be well to give him a touch of the question; fire and the rack are great persuaders."

"Cethegus," said Catilina, sternly, "once and for all understand that I will not torture my slaves at your bidding. Before I do that, I will abandon the entire plot."

And Cethegus subsided, growling.

Thus the argument went on until well past midnight, with recriminations and quarrels in plenty, Catilina finally putting an end to it with:

"This profits nothing; it is plain that we shall get nowhere this way, and we will do better to give our time to a discussion of what should be done."

This opened another debate. Coeparius was for abandoning the whole conspiracy, but the others cried him down, insisting that the affair go on.

"Two things are clear," pointed out Catilina. "Three, in fact. First, that Cicero will not move against us before we have openly declared ourselves, or at least given him the evidence he desires. This last, with proper precautions, we can avoid doing until the affair is ripe. Second, that we must continue to strengthen ourselves within the City. And third, that we must change the date for the uprising, since he doubtless knows our present plans. Manlius, of course, should move at once on Praeneste, to occupy it before Metellus Celer can do so, and I will charge myself with sending word to him. As for the date, I am for setting a later one; in that case, finding the appointed time to pass without Cicero's prophecy being fulfilled, the praetors and tribunes will relax their vigilance, and may even discredit his tale entirely."

Cethegus, always rash and headstrong, was for breaking out at once, and the debate was renewed, though on a fresh subject. But no conclusion was reached, and at length it grew so far along into the morning hours that the meeting broke up, having decided no more than that Statilius, Cethegus, Annius, and some others were to continue fomenting rebellion among the slaves and idlers of the City, and that the final date would be fixed at a later meeting.

As the conspirators were leaving, Fulvia approached me.

"My Red-head," she began, "I am going to ask Catilina to let you escort me home. Pugnax is lame from a fall and could not accompany me to-night, and on arriving here I dismissed my bodyguard lest they be tempted to spy on us. I counted on Curius to see me home, but for reasons of his own he cannot. Will it be too great a hardship, Red-head?"

I bowed.

"It will be a pleasure, *Domina*," I told her, perhaps not quite truthfully, for I was tired. "And even were it not, who am I, a slave, to complain?"

"You and your courtly words!" she mocked. "Where did you learn to make fair speeches—in Dumnorix' school?"

"They come naturally to my lips when I talk with you," I answered, bowing again, whereat she laughed lightly.

"I know well you are a privileged character," she teased. "So privileged, in truth, that I am half afraid to trust myself to you lest you kidnap me and carry me off to some cave in the Sabine Hills."

"It is indeed a temptation, *Domina*," I chaffed her, whereat she laughed again, and tapped me on the arm with her fan. I would never have dared speak thus to Sempronia or to any true patrician dame, but Fulvia, for all her good birth, was without dignity, laughing and joking freely with her slaves.

My master readily gave the desired permission, and we set out, she talking and jesting with me as though we were equals, holding my arm and snuggling against me as she might have done with one of her own class, and little dreaming how her manner disgusted me. One may be conscious of his own worth, yet at the same time realize the vast social gulf that is fixed between a patrician and a slave, and the high-born person who of his own will steps across that gulf must always forfeit the slave's respect; it is possible to be kind and courteous without loss of dignity. However, there is for many women a glamour surrounding a successful gladiator, and Fulvia doubtless was one of these.

She told me that Pugnax was not seriously hurt, but had merely twisted an ankle, and since the dawn was lightening the east when we reached our goal, I asked if I might not see him.

"Certainly," she replied. "Come in."

A Slave of Catiline

We entered—after rousing the doorkeeper from slumber—and found Polla asleep on a marble bench in the *atrium*. Fulvia woke her, saying:

"Conduct Tiberius to Pugnax' sleeping-chamber, then attend me. My Red-head, I leave you in good hands. Farewell." And she went to her own room.

Polla and I exchanged a few words on the way to Pugnax' quarters, which, like most of the sleeping-rooms, were on the western side of the *peristylium,* then she left me and hurried off to Fulvia, while I pushed back the curtain and went in.

Pugnax was not asleep—he told me that his cursed ankle had kept him so much in bed, the past two days, that he was wholly slept out—and after greeting me joyfully he demanded the latest news. I told him of the debate in the Senate, whereof he had heard only rumors, and I then related what had passed at Catilina's home. Pugnax whistled softly.

"Ha, my Tiberius," he said, whimsically, "I begin to have qualms. Cicero may come from Arpinum, from the Volscian Hills, but he is no rustic; he knows his way about! It is no slight feat for a *novus homo,* one of the equestrian order, to lift himself to the consulship. And if he has turned that brain of his on us—*Mehercle,* I can see a row of crosses decorating the Via Appia, and on them you and I and many others."

"Not our confederates," I told him.

"No," he admitted. "They are patricians, and will not be crucified. But Manlius' army and the City slaves would make almost as brave a show as did the men of Spartacus. *Euge!* It pleases me not at all!"

I shrugged my shoulders.

"The Fates will send what They regard as proper," I told him. "At least there can be no turning back now. And if we succeed we shall be justified of all men."

" 'If,' " he remarked, dryly. "Two mighty letters! In your opinion, who is the traitor?"

I shook my head.

"So far as I can guess, it might be anyone."

"I would most quickly suspect Coeparius," he mused, "save that were he faithless he would now be on his way to Athens or Alexandria; he lacks the cold courage to face Catilina and Vargunteius and Cethegus after betraying them. Titus Volturcius, too, is a weakling; he might be the one."

There came a knock at the doorway.

"Enter!" cried Pugnax, and in response to his summons the drapery was lifted and Polla stepped in, hooking the curtain back that the morning sun might illuminate the room.

"Fulvia sleeps," she told us. "And having had

a nap while waiting for her, I am not sleepy. So I thought to have a word with my brother."

"And your lover," I laughed, whereat she blushed most charmingly; all prejudice aside, she was an attractive girl, and I could not blame Pugnax for falling victim to her sweet face and pretty ways.

"Tell her what you have just told me," he suggested, and as I raised my eyebrows in surprise, "Oh, she is abreast of all that has gone before. Yesterday she suspected, asked questions, and trapped me—the little witch!" he added, half proudly, pleased with her acumen.

It seemed to me that he had scarcely acted the part of wisdom, and I thought of the oath he had sworn. But after all, he was deeply in love, and must share his hopes and fears with the object of his affection. And Polla was no chatterbox, but could keep a secret with anyone.

So I repeated my tale, standing the while in the doorway, that none might approach unseen. Polla listened thoughtfully, biting her finger as though to fasten her attention. When I had finished:

"I know who has betrayed you," she said.

"In the name of Mercury, who?" demanded Pugnax and I together.

She pointed her finger toward the front of the house.

"You mean—"

She nodded. Instinctively I lowered my voice. "Fulvia?"

Again Polla nodded, and with an oath I clapped my hand on my dagger. Polla sprang and caught my arm.

"No, no!" she cried. "I do not mean intentionally. But you know she is given to loose talk, and more than once I have heard her boasting to her friends of the jewels and riches that her lover Curius will heap upon her when a certain mysterious event comes to pass. Word of this has got back to Cicero, and he, being no fool, has put two and two together and set spies on Curius."

Pugnax and I looked at each other, he narrowing his eyes and pursing his lips while Polla spoke. Then he nodded slowly.

"She has the answer," he said. "The child is right."

"Per Deos Immortales!" I burst out. "Catilina must know of this at once." Pugnax nodded agreement. "Do you two keep silent," I told them, and once more he nodded, while Polla rather scornfully answered:

"Of course!"

Bidding them an abrupt farewell, I made my way out of the house and set off post-haste for home.

CHAPTER V

Of the Plan for the Saturnalia; and the Plot to Slay the Consul

CATILINA heard my news in silence. At first his expressive countenance glowed with fierce anger, but this settled ere long into a resigned disgust. When I had finished:

"It is what comes of taking women into a plot like ours," he said. "It was a mistake, and the Gods know I fought against it, but Curius—oh, well, the harm is done, and it remains now to repair it as best we may."

The next few days were uneventful; no further attack by the consul followed, nor did the conspirators move openly. To be sure, we were busy with various secret affairs, not least of which was our persistent recruiting, and Catilina sent Pugnax to spread disaffection in Dumnorix' school—rather, to increase it, for the seeds had long since been sown. I never learned the details of my friend's work there, but I knew that he took into his confidence a number of the gladiators with whom he was particularly well acquainted, and that they received the news with pleasure, making plans to rush the gate when the appointed time came. And, of course, there was no doubt that the others would join the revolt as soon as it broke out; Dumnorix ruled by fear, not love.

It was an anxious time for us all, and I know that I myself had much trouble in keeping an even mind. Not that I dreaded the event; I had faced death too often to fear to look him in the eyes. But the strain of waiting, of wondering whether or not the consul had seen through all our plans, of wondering what would be his next move, and how we could frustrate it—this kept us all on edge. Even Catilina, usually calm and equable, grew snappish and irritable for the first time since I had known him; he had a slave whipped for spilling a cup of wine, though the fault was purely an accident, the result of a stumble. Of course, with many Roman masters, this would be nothing out of the way, but so exceptional was it with Catilina that I mention it as indicating his frame of mind. And the tension was no little increased when word came to us that Manlius had taken the field, as ordered; thereafter we waited, more on edge than before, to hear that he had occupied Praeneste, for that would mean that he was within twenty-five miles— a good day's march—of Rome.

A large proportion of the senators were out of sympathy with the consul, resenting whatever he might do. These great families, being the patrician class, claimed descent from the original founders of Latium, the Iulian gens even going so far as to trace their line back to Aeneas, and through him to Venus, to which goddess the greatest of all the family afterward built a temple, dedicating it to Venus Genetrix. The rise of the equestrian order, who in the main controlled the wealth of the City, was a matter of fear and hatred to these patricians, the office-holding class, who saw their ancient privileges threatened as the knights grew in power; and since the consul was the greatest of all equestrians, and further, since he was born without the City, it follows that nothing he did could find favor in the eyes of the jealous patricians. It will, of course, be understood that I am speaking in general terms; there were some patricians, such as Marcus Cato and Gaius Caesar, who sought the welfare of the State rather than their own profit.

One result of this party hatred was that the majority of the patricians believed my master a wholly innocent and much abused person. Here was one of their own class, a member of the noble Sergian gens, accused of the vilest treason—as it seemed to them—against his own order; accused, further, by an equestrian, a *novus homo,* whose house could show no waxen busts of curule ancestors. What more natural than for these nobles to side with their own class against the hated equestrian consul? And Catilina had stood for the consulship against Cicero, being defeated by only a small vote, so what more natural than for patrician jealousy to read equestrian jealousy in Cicero's words?

My master resolved to take advantage of this feeling and if possible to strengthen it. To that end he went of his own free will to various magistrates, offering himself as a prisoner, but one after another refused to accept his offer. From the most ancient times, Rome has never imprisoned as a punishment, so we have no prison; the Carcer of Ancus Martius is no more than a place of detention for those awaiting trial. Small, ill fitted, and foul, it is no fit habitation for a noble, and any magistrate receiving a prisoner must keep him as a guest. It was not from reluctance to entertain my master that the praetors declined to take him in, but from fear of what his friends, who were also their friends, would say. However, Catilina persisted, and at length Marcus Metellus consented to receive him.

"Your captivity will be light, my Sergius," said the praetor. "I am not in sympathy with this upstart consul, nor do I find it easy to credit that you are planning to burn and loot Rome and slaughter your fellow patricians. We will observe the form of captivity, but I will set no guard over you, and you are free to come and go as you like."

Catilina thanked him, gave me orders for the conduct of his household, and took up his dwelling with Metellus.

Thus matters stood until the day following the Nones of November,* when a meeting of the conspirators was called at Marcus Laeca's. Again my master and I took our way to the well-remembered Street of the Scythe-Makers, and this time Pugnax stood guard at the door while I climbed to my familiar perch on the roof.

"I have some things to say to-night which will not bear overhearing, my Tiberius," Catilina told me. "Therefore you will guard against eavesdroppers. Laeca, it is a cool night; may I beg a cup of wine to warm and hearten our guards for their vigil?"

Laeca smiled and clapped his hands, and a slave entered, to be sent for two cups of wine. Returning, he handed them to Pugnax and me, whereupon we splashed out a few drops to the Gods of the household, and dipped our noses into the goblets. It was the choicest Caecuban, undiluted, and flowed down our throats like liquid gold. Pugnax looked at me over the brim of the cup and I returned the

* November 6.

look. Handing the empty vessel back to the slave, he sighed and remarked:

"*Per Bacchum!* Give me but three such drinks, *Domine,* and I will sack Rome single-handed! The Gods pity the spy who falls to-night into my hands; I will eat him alive. Come, my Tiberius; we are well fortified against the cold."

We took our places, and I found great interest in watching the plotters as they arrived, for I squatted at the rear of the *impluvium* and could see them in the room beneath me. The strain of the past few days had told on them, increasing their nervousness and graving deep lines of worry on their features. Fulvia's hands were more fluttery than ever; Coeparius could not sit still, but paced restlessly up and down until Cethegus cursed him into a chair; Curius shared Fulvia's nervousness; and Lentulus Sura had lost much of his fat, so that his cheeks hung flabby and pendulous about his jaw.

"A pretty lot of conspirators!" I thought to myself, looking them over. "It needs but an aedile knocking on the door, and we would see them hiding under chairs and tables. And I would bet five *denarii* to two that Volturcius would take refuge in the pond! How dare such sheep conspire?"

To do them justice, though, not all were so visibly disturbed. My master, of course, and Sempronia, were calm as ever, while Vargunteius, Annius, Cornelius, Laeca, and Publius Umbrenus—this last the only freedman among us—retained at least an outward composure. More or less conversation went on while they awaited the others, and I heard Lentulus remark to Annius:

"What think you of the many omens and portents of the past few days, my Quintus? Do they foretell our success or our failure? Which?"

"I am not vastly concerned with omens," Annius returned. "I hold, with Terentius Afer, that Fortuna helps the brave."

"But, Quintus, these were omens of the gravest," Lentulus expostulated, in evident agitation. "Surely you do not deny that the Gods thus indicate to men Their will? Why, yesterday the statues in the Forum were seen to sweat, one day last week a cow in the Forum Boarium gave birth to a six-legged calf, and no longer ago than to-day a chicken, sacrificed to Mercury, proved to have no heart!"

"Bah!" snorted Annius. "Did you with your own eyes behold these marvels?"

"No-o," Lentulus admitted, reluctantly. "But they are the talk of the City."

"Together with many another old wives' tale."

"Quintus, do you deny the Gods?"

"No," replied Annius, forcibly. "But I deny that They are fools. I deny that They amuse Themselves with tricks like those the priests of Isis use to impose on the vulgar."

Lentulus was shocked, and would have remonstrated, but now all were present, and Catilina rose to address them.

"I have news," he said, and at once all eyes were turned on him. He looked about the assemblage, and smiled faintly. "A courier reached me this afternoon from Manlius, to say that Metellus Celer has justified his name* and has occupied Praeneste before Manlius reached the place."

Fulvia let out a startled cry, then clapped her hand over her mouth; and Lentulus fetched up a groan from the depths of his boots, while the faces of all showed grave concern.

"But . . . but . . . Catilina," stammered Titus Volturcius. "That means death to our plans!"

Catilina eyed him sardonically.

"Not at all," he answered. "It means only that we must change them. Instead of coming into the City from Praeneste, Manlius will come in through Janiculum—that is all."

"And have a hostile army in his rear," commented Nobilior.

"What of it?" Catilina demanded.

"Simply this: that Celer, returning from Praeneste, will enter the City at the same time, and we

---

* Celer means swift.

shall have twenty thousand men fighting in the streets."

"Again, what of it? Did you expect to take Rome peacefully? And if our men cannot match Celer's levies in the hole-and-corner business of street fighting, we deserve to lose."

Volturcius got to his feet; he was shaking like a leaf in the wind, and could hardly speak.

"I . . . I cannot go on," he stammered. "This news . . . the omens . . . surely the Gods are angry with us. . . . Catilina, I withdraw . . . I . . . I . . . no, it is hopeless . . . the Gods . . . the Gods. . . ."

At a nod from Catilina, Vargunteius and Annius placed themselves between Volturcius and the door, and drew their daggers, while Cethegus, steel in hand, approached the trembling man.

"You are too deep in our secrets to desert us now, Volturcius," said Catilina, smoothly. "Either you remain in our company, remain true to us, or your body, pierced and looted by thieves, is found in some dark lane of the Subura. Choose!"

Volturcius looked wildly about, then with a gasping cry buried his face in his hands and dropped into his chair.

"Choose!" repeated Catilina, and Volturcius gave a choking promise.

"I . . . I will . . . remain," he sobbed.

"Best let me finish him," Cethegus advised. "If we let him live he will betray us. See how he shakes! Has he the courage to withstand the rack and the fire?"

"Take him outside to despatch him," Laeca requested. "I have had a new floor laid here within the month."

Cethegus grasped Volturcius by the neck and jerked him to his feet, whereupon the terrified wretch broke loose and groveled on the floor, begging for mercy.

"I will be true!" he howled. "By all the Gods I swear it! I will, I will! Pity! Have pity!"

"And this thing calls itself a Roman!" exclaimed Sempronia, with utter contempt. "I could make a stouter one of straw!"

"Enough!" said Catilina. "Let him go, Gaius. Titus, get up and take your seat."

"You are making a mistake," insisted Cethegus. "Best finish him; it is but the stroke of a dagger. Soon or late, if he lives, he will betray us."

"On my head be it," Catilina replied. "The Fates will hold but scant good fortune for us, once we start slaughtering one another. Let him rise."

Cethegus growled, but obeyed, and Volturcius resumed his place. He was not, however, entirely reassured, but kept an uneasy eye on Cethegus.

"We must revise our plans to some extent," my

master said. "It was planned, as you all know, to have the uprising take place day after to-morrow. But since Manlius is cut off from Praeneste, and since the consul has knowledge of our scheme, it will be necessary to postpone the revolt somewhat. Meanwhile we can be strengthening ourselves. What date would you suggest?"

Cethegus leaped to his feet.

"I am against a postponement," he declared, savagely. "We have already put it off once, and I crave to get to work. I say go ahead as planned —day after to-morrow."

"Your proposal is madness," Laeca objected. "Manlius cannot get here in time, and we shall have Celer upon our backs at once. And how can the slaves and gladiators withstand two legions of disciplined soldiers, fully armed? Cethegus, you are a fool."

"A fool, am I?" Cethegus whirled and advanced upon Laeca, head thrust forward, brutal face lowering with rage. "A fool, eh?"

"Yes," snapped Catilina. "Laeca is right; you are. Sit down."

Cethegus glared at the leader.

Sit down!" repeated Catilina, the rasp of authc cy in his voice, and Cethegus, overawed, obeyed.

"Now as to date," my master went on, but Cornelius interrupted.

"Why not the Feast of the Saturnalia?" he asked.

"Too long," Cethegus growled. "Too long to wait."

"Six weeks from to-night," responded Cornelius. "A long time to wait in suspense, I grant, but consider the advantages. There will be the usual games and feasting, the public mind will be given over to merry-making, and best of all, it is the time when slaves and masters change places for three days, the latter obeying the former in all things. Consider the advantage that gives the slaves. Why, it is revolt made easy!"

Some debate followed, Cethegus being the chief objector, but in the end Cornelius' idea was adopted, and it was decided that we should make our great stroke on the Saturnalia.

For myself, I was none too well satisfied. It seemed to me that a revolt of this kind should be sharp and sudden, that the plans should be quickly laid and swiftly carried out; and I felt that this temporizing, these repeated delays, did not augur well for our success. They represented, I thought, a weakness, but my position as a slave would hardly let me oppose my own ideas to those of the others, and I kept silence.

"There is something else," said Vargunteius, when at last the date was approved. "I feel that the army is the more important weapon of the two;

more valuable than the revolt within the City." The others nodded agreement. "That being so," he continued, "it is of the utmost consequence that it be officered as well as possible. Now, granting that Manlius is a good leader, I feel that Catilina is a better; he is more experienced, more crafty, more forceful, and the men will follow him more loyally. Would it not be well for him to place himself at the head of the army? We others can manage affairs within the gates."

A debate on this point ensued, Coeparius, Lentulus, and Volturcius holding out for my master's presence in Rome, but in the end it was decided that he should join Manlius, Catilina himself ending the discussion; he told me, on the way home, that he had decided on that course before Vargunteius spoke.

Sempronia had an idea to offer.

"There are in Rome," she pointed out, "certain envoys from the Allobroges, nearest of the tribes of Gallia Transalpina. They come to lay their grievances before the Senate, seeking relief from usurious tribal debts owed to money-lenders of the City. Why not promise them the relief they crave, in return for their assistance? They could well furnish us horsemen, and if we treat with them at once their cavalry could be here in time to aid us in our enterprise."

This also was discussed, and the idea met with general favor.

"Does anyone here know these envoys?" Catilina asked, and Umbrenus the freedman replied:

"I know one of them."

"Could you not introduce yourself to the others, and present them to one of our company, who will gain their confidence?"

"Assuredly," Umbrenus answered. "It is a simple matter."

"Do so, then." Catilina looked about the room. "Gabinius Capito," he said, "do you have the matter in charge. Take what steps you think desirable, promise the Allobroges whatever they wish, and secure their adherence."

Capito nodded, and with Umbrenus retired to a corner to discuss ways and means.

I looked for the meeting to break up, but Catilina, it seemed, had a further matter to present, and at his next words I well-nigh fell through the *impluvium* with mingled astonishment and horror.

"One thing more," he said. "It is wholly out of the question for me to betake myself to the army and at the same time leave behind me in the City so venomous a foe as our consul, Cicero. Steps must be taken to abate his enmity; I dare not leave the urban revolt in charge of any but myself so long as he interests himself in our plans."

"What would you suggest?" inquired Lentulus Sura. "Can his friendship be gained? Can he be bought off with promises?"

There was a general laugh at this, even the dour Cethegus relaxing into a smile.

"No," replied Catilina, in tones of sarcasm. "No, unfortunately, my Lentulus, he cannot. There is but one way. It will require two men. Who will volunteer?"

By this time I was fairly sick, and I use the word in no rhetorical sense; an actual feeling of nausea pervaded my body. Cicero, the foremost man of the State, he who by sheer power of his mighty brain had lifted himself from obscurity to the highest position in all the world—such a one to fall before the daggers of assassins! The man who had denied the Roman mob their wish in order to grant me the life of my friend—he to be struck down like a mangy dog! Then and there it came home to me what conspiracy meant; before that time I had known, of course, that many men would die in order to bring about our success, but the realization had been vague. And in any case they were men whose lives held no great interest for me. This, though, was different, and the vision shocked me through and through, and I began to see what a foul thing I was, with what foul men I had associated myself. I thought of the thieves of the Subura whom Cati-

lina and I had slain, and I asked myself wherein we
were better than they. They slew by stealth, at
midnight, for money—what else were we about to
do? Am I one to despise them? I asked myself.
Were they one whit worse than I, who call myself
a man? And the soul within me answered, "No!"

But I was fond of my master; could I betray him?
He had taken me from the hell of Dumnorix' school,
he had befriended me, had raised me to a position
above that of most slaves, had treated me with kindness. Could I repay this with treachery? And I
had sworn secrecy—what of my oath? It was no
easy choice, and dropping my face in my hands I
groaned aloud; fortunately, the conspirators were
so engrossed in their plan that they did not hear me.
Then Vargunteius spoke.

"I will be one," he offered. It was what I might
have expected; Vargunteius lacked the savagery of
Cethegus, but he owned a cool, poised courage that
the more headlong brute did not possess.

"I will be the other." This from Cornelius, and
again I was not surprised; they two were the best
of all the conspirators, leaving aside my master.

"That is well," I heard Catilina say. "The best
time will be in the morning, when he receives his
clients; then he will be least on guard, least sur-
rounded by friends. I leave the matter in your

hands, my Lucius, my Gaius. Fix your own plans, your method of approach, and strike quick and strike hard."

"We will attend when he receives his clients, as you say," Vargunteius agreed. "Eh, Gaius?" Cornelius nodded assent. "We will devise some pretext to gain admittance, and by the third hour you shall have news that he is dead."

All the company save Catilina touched some form of metal about their persons, to avert the evil omen of the mention of death. But my master, free from all superstition, did not do so. I? Well, I cannot truly say that I believe in such things—yet it is well to have the signs favorable.

This last suggestion, however, was entirely too much for me. Cicero had a daughter Tullia, a charming little maid of some five years, bright, eager, and altogether delightful; I had more than once observed her in the Argiletum, clinging to her father's hand and chatting and laughing merrily with him as he moved among the book-shops; it was plain that she adored him, and he, her. She would undoubtedly be in the *atrium* when he received his clients; was she to see her beloved father slaughtered before her very eyes, that she might bear that terrible vision with her through life? I have always been fond of children—in that respect I am a true Roman—and this seemed to me a refinement of cruelty; far worse than to strike him down in the Curia, in the presence of grown men.

Now the meeting was breaking up, and my master summoned me. Twisting around, I grasped the edge of the *impluvium,* swung, and dropped, taking care that my swing carried me clear of the basin. Fulvia jumped and gave a little scream, then checked herself and giggled shamefacedly.

"I thought—I thought it was an aedile, come to arrest us," she apologized, and the others laughed at her, though with a strained note in their mirth.

"Yes, *Domine,*" I saluted, and Catilina replied:

"Attend me home."

Neither of us spoke much on the way to Metellus' house; Catilina was doubtless revolving plans in his mind, and I was fully occupied with wondering what I should do. As I left him he said:

"My Tiberius, things move. In another two months, if all goes well, you can call yourself a free man. And doubt not that loyalty to me shall be richly rewarded."

"I have no such doubts, *Domine,*" I told him. "Good-night."

He disappeared within, and I took myself off.

Not home, however. I had too much on my mind to let me sleep, and I hurried to Fulvia's house, demanding to see Pugnax. This time the door-keeper admitted me without question—having in mind what the chief of Fulvia's bodyguard had said on a former occasion—and I went direct to my friend's room. He was asleep, but woke and had me by the throat when I touched his shoulder. His dagger-point was at my heart, but when I said, "Tiberius," he relaxed.

"Per Martes!" he swore, astonished. "You lacked but a hair of joining your ancestors. What brings you here at this hour? Wait; I will strike a light." He fumbled about. "Where is that cursed flint?"

"No light," I stopped him. "Sit here while I unfold a tale."

Side by side on the bed, I put my lips close to his ear and in a whisper that could not have been heard three feet away I told the latest decision of the conspirators.

"Per Deos Immortales!" he exclaimed in an undertone, when I had finished. "Cicero, eh? Well, he will not be the first to fall at the hands of daggermen. Nor the last, perchance."

"The question is, are we going to allow it, you and I?"

"But what can we do? Can we two confront the plotters and forbid them this thing? The dogs of the Esquiline would gnaw our bones, or the fish of Tiber-mouth hold high revel."

"Yet we must do something! It was Cicero who

spared you when all Rome clamored for your death. Shall he be allowed to fall before the daggers of assassins?"

"We might lie in wait for Vargunteius and Cornelius as they leave their homes, and slay them ourselves," Pugnax offered. "On such an errand they will doubtless go unescorted."

"It will be daylight," I pointed out. "And we would unquestionably be seen and recognized. Then we would die without aiding Cicero, for it would simply mean that others would take their places."

"True," he admitted. "And the same thing holds if we should make our way into their houses and strike them as they sleep. Further, I could not find Cornelius' sleeping-chamber in the dark; I do not know his house. Do you?"

"No. And in any case, the plan is useless."

"Well, what then? There is naught we can do."

"Listen, Pugnax! How if we went to Cicero's home and warned him of the danger?"

"In the name of Mercury, my Tiberius! Have you taken leave of your senses? Can you vision what would happen to a pair of slaves who went to the consul admitting complicity in a plot to destroy Rome and overthrow the State with fire and sword? The public artificers would receive orders to prepare two neat crosses, which you and I would decorate, much against my will, whatever you may desire."

"You say truth," I conceded. "But for all that it is in my mind to go to Cicero. A life demands a life, and further, I say frankly, my Pugnax, I cannot stomach this thing. I have seen men die in the arena, and have brought about the death of some few, myself, but not men who have given me the life of my only friend, when all hope was gone." I flung my arm about his shoulders. "I do not ask you to come with me; indeed, I would prefer that you do not; it is enough that one of us die. But I do wish you to know my reason; I would not have you think it mere wanton treachery on my part. Remain here, my Pugnax, and return to your slumbers. Farewell, my friend; we shall meet in the Elysian Fields." I gave him a final hug and rose to go.

But he caught me by the tunic.

"Tiberius," he whispered, "there are times when I am certain your mother dropped you on your head in childhood. Am I the man to let you undertake this errand alone? Have I ever shown myself either a coward or false to friendship? If you are crucified, so am I. Besides," he added, whimsically, "I have always had a desire to look down upon the world from an exalted position. Let me but find my clothes, and I am with you."

He dressed hurriedly, by sense of touch, then left me for a moment, and returning, said:

"The *clepsydra* * gives but five hours to dawn; we shall do well to hasten."

"How could you tell?" I asked curiously. "You could not see it."

He chuckled.

"When laid up with my ankle I learned to tell time in the dark. I thrust my finger into the overflow pan; the water came up to the last joint. Here, take my hand and follow; I know this garden as I know my room. We will go secretly, by the back way; it were a shame to disturb the *janitor's* slumber—further, he is much given to wonderment, and I would not agitate his feeble mind."

There was no moon, and the outlines of the roof showed merely as forms of blackness against the blue of the sky; I could vaguely see the white of the marble columns gleaming faint in the dark, but of details in the garden I could make out nothing, and I feared to crack my shins over some marble bench, or topple some urn or bust from its pedestal with a crash that would wake the household. But Pugnax must have had the eyes of a cat, for he led me with a sure step along the colonnade to the foot of the garden, where a door opened on another street. Fulvia's house extended from street to street, but

---

* Water-clock.

the rooms did not run all around the *peristylium,* and at the bottom there was but a wall some ten feet high. Pugnax fumbled at the door.

"Naturally!" he said in disgust. "The slave who has the gate in charge must select this night of all nights to be conscientious. Well, over the wall. You first, being lighter."

He bent over, and I stepped from his back to his shoulders, to catch the top of the wall and pull myself up. Turning around, I made myself into an inverted U, belly down on the wall, legs hanging over the street and arm extended to Pugnax. Three times he sprang, missing my hand in the darkness, but the fourth time he caught it, and with straining muscles I lifted until he gripped the wall with both hands and swung up beside me. Then dropping to the pavement, we set out for Cicero's home, a few blocks away.

The City was dark as Pluto's realm, though off in the direction of the Forum Boarium and the Forum Olitorium, where the country folk were bringing in produce for the day's markets, there was in the sky a glow of torch-light that still further enhanced the likeness to the world below. But we knew our streets, and pressed rapidly onward.

Once, from a doorway, three men rushed at us, two bearing daggers and the third a torch. Pugnax and I laughed aloud, drew our daggers, and sprang

to meet them, whereat the torch-bearer cried in
sudden fear:

"Back! Back! It is Tiberius and Pugnax!" And
the three incontinently took to their heels. A reputation from the arena is at times no bad thing to
have.

No others interfered with us, and in less than
quarter of an hour from leaving Fulvia's we were
knocking at Cicero's door, demanding admittance of
the *janitor*, who rubbed his eyes and growled at
being roused from slumber.

CHAPTER VI

Of My Mother; and How I Transferred My Allegiance

CICERO'S doorkeeper flatly refused to admit us, for which, as I now look back upon the matter, I cannot blame him. But at the time I was more than angry; my agitation of mind, together with the knowledge that I was giving my life to save the consul's, made me furious, and I hurled my weight against the door, slamming it open and throwing the *janitor* across the vestibule. A huge fawn-colored Molossian dog was fastened to the wall, and he went into a rage of barking, leaping the length of his chain to get at Pugnax and me. The doorkeeper rushed to this brute.

"Out with you!" he cried to us. "Out! Or I loose the dog on you." And he tried to release the chain.

But the dog's frantic plunges kept the man from undoing the hook, and I sprang upon him, dragging him away from the beast. My hand on his throat, my dagger-point at his stomach, I forced the *janitor* back against the wall.

"Fool!" I snarled. "Ass! Dolt! We have come

128

to save your master from dagger-men—and you deny us entrance! Do you crave to see him murdered?" I lifted my voice. "Ho, Marcus Tullius!" I bellowed. "Ho, Marcus Tullius Cicero! Here is your *janitor* who wishes to see you slain!" Even in my excitement I was forced to smile at the way the poor wretch's eyes goggled and his jaw dropped at this announcement; his hands fluttered a protest, but he was too frightened to make it a hearty one, and he dared not resist.

My outcry was scarcely needed; the noise of the scuffle, with the barking of the dog and the clashing of his chain, had roused the household, and a score of slaves poured into the *atrium,* some with daggers, but most armed with heavy cudgels. I could foresee a stormy time ahead; they would be little apt to argue the matter with us. So I caught the *janitor's* neck in the crook of my right elbow, swung him about to bring his back toward me, and with my dagger over his heart I backed against the wall, using him as a shield; by now I had worked my way from the vestibule into the *atrium* itself, Pugnax at my heels. Foremost among the slaves was Cicero's librarian, Tiro, for this man, though but newly come from Greece, already worshipped his master, and would unhesitatingly have given his life to save the consul's. And it is understating the case to say that Cicero was fond of Tiro; there was a strong affection between them, wherefore Pugnax showed excellent judgment in seizing the librarian and using him as I was doing with the doorkeeper.

Seeing Tiro and the *janitor* thus endangered, the others came to an abrupt halt, and before anything else could be done, the consul appeared from his bed-chamber. He had hastily wrapped a blanket about himself, and his long, thin neck and lean shanks protruded grotesquely from its folds.

"What is wrong?" he inquired, raising his voice to make it heard above the raving of the dog, and at once all the slaves began to talk. He motioned them to silence and repeated his question.

"*Domine*," I said, "my friend and I have come hither to warn you that your life is in danger from assassins. Your *janitor* would not admit us, so we forced our way in."

"Most likely they themselves are the assassins," spoke up the major-domo. "The red-haired one is Catilina's chief of bodyguard, and a former gladiator. And they are both armed."

"Protect us against your slaves, oh Consul," I said, and cast my dagger on the floor, at the same time releasing the doorkeeper, who promptly put a good distance between himself and me. "There is my evidence of good faith." Pugnax freed Tiro, and threw down his own dagger.

By this time a number of other persons had ap-

peared from the sleeping-chambers, among them
Terentia, Cicero's wife, with some friend of hers
whom I did not know; Tullia, round-eyed and wondering, clung to her mother's garment, half hiding
behind Terentia, and from that refuge peered curiously at us.

"I would turn them over to the praetor," said
Terentia, a harsh-voiced, domineering woman. "Fire
and the rack will get the truth from them."

"Not so, my dear," objected Cicero, mildly.
"They come of their own free will; that much is
plain." He looked attentively at me. "Where have
I seen that red head of yours?" he asked.

"In the arena, *Domine,*" I told him. "Some
months back, at Piso's games, you were good enough
to grant me the life of my friend, here. I was a
retiarius of Dumnorix' school."

He shook his head.

"Longer ago than that," he said. "Your features are somehow familiar to me, though I cannot
identify the memory. Well, no matter. What is
your tale? Silence that brute," he added, and one
of the slaves, stepping to the vestibule, commanded
the dog to lie down and be quiet. "What is your
tale?" the consul repeated.

"With deference, *Domine,* I would relate it less
publicly." And I glanced about at the company.
I observed that Terentia's friend, a dignified, hand-

some blonde of about forty years, with a fine patrician air, was regarding me closely, but I thought nothing of it, for a hubbub of protest broke out at my suggestion. The burden of the clamor was to the effect that I was trying to get the consul alone that I might slay him, having been frustrated in my first attempt.

Cicero has often been accused of personal cowardice, but I must say that on this occasion he gave no evidence thereof. It would be natural enough for a student, a man of books, to show less courage than a soldier or a gladiator, but the consul displayed no qualms whatever. Having succeeded in quieting the commotion, he yielded to the solicitations of his family so far as to have Pugnax and me searched for other weapons, but when none was found he dismissed the slaves and led us to his private office adjoining the *atrium;* Terentia and her friend remained to talk the matter over, and Tullia —the darling!—was frightened at the peril to her father, so Tiro took her on his knee to comfort her.

Cicero's house was small, but for the most part beautifully decorated with the finest imaginable statuary, paintings, mosaics—art work of all kinds. The office, however, was severely plain, holding nothing but three chairs, a cabinet for books, and a small table on which were a lamp, some pens, and an ink-stand. The consul seated himself, Pugnax and I of course standing, and when he had sat down he turned to me.

"You seem to be the leader in this matter," he said. "Now, what is your news?"

"Domine," I answered, respectfully, "I am chief of bodyguard to Lucius Sergius Catilina; my friend, here, enjoys the same position with Fulvia. Partly as a result of our positions, and partly for other causes, we have become privy to the conspiracy of which you already know so much." He nodded. "But what you do not know is that last night, at a meeting of the plotters, it was decided that you should be assassinated. Two of the conspirators— Lucius Vargunteius and Gaius Cornelius—volunteered for the deed, and will attend for the purpose when you receive your clients this morning."

"This is true?" he asked, sternly.

"By the spirits of my fathers, it is true."

Cicero thought for a moment, then clapped his hands, the major-domo entering immediately.

"Sextus," said the consul, "go with all speed to Gaius Caesar and ask him to arm and come here at once. Say it is a matter of life and death. Send a trusty slave on the same errand to my brother Quintus, another to Marcus Cato, and a third to Lucius Flaccus the praetor. With all speed!"

The major-domo bowed and withdrew, and Cicero turned again to Pugnax and me.

"Domine," I answered, "I am chief of body-guard to Lucius Sergius Catilina."

"You are both slaves?" he inquired.

"Yes, *Domine.*"

"You know what slaves may expect when they conspire against the State?"

"Yes, *Domine,*" we both answered, steadily.

"How comes it, then, that you place yourselves in my hands, asking me to crucify you? Do you think I will neglect my duty?"

"No, *Domine,*" I assured him. "We expect the cross. But for two years I was a gladiator in Dumnorix' school. The only friend I had there, one whom I loved and still love as a brother, was this man beside me. Greatly against our will, we were matched to fight, and Fortuna aided me. As always, the mob clamored for his life, but you were acting as *editor,* Piso being sick, and when I appealed to you, you ordered my friend to be spared. A life demands a life, and since you gave me his, I have saved yours. That is all; what comes after does not concern the matter."

Cicero turned to Pugnax.

"Where do you figure in the affair?" he queried. "Why do you also offer yourself in sacrifice?"

"Could I let my friend come alone on such an errand?" said Pugnax, returning the consul's look with a steady eye.

"H'm!" said Cicero. "Well, you are brave men. It grieves me to——" A knock at the door interrupted him. "Enter!" he called, and Terentia and her friend came in.

"Marcus," said the former, "Flava wishes to speak with you."

The consul rose and offered them chairs, and when they were settled the blonde matron began.

"It is not properly with you I wish to talk," she told Cicero, "but with your informant; this man who has come so strangely to the house."

"By all means," the consul told her, courteously, and she turned to me.

"What is your name?" she asked.

"Tiberius, *Domina.*"

"Your parents gave you that name?"

"My foster-parents, *Domina.* I was cast ashore from a shipwreck on the sunrise coast of Italia, not far from Cannae, and a fisherman adopted me. Finding about my neck a gold *bulla* marked TIB, he took my name to be Tiberius, and so called me. All the others on the vessel perished in the wreck, so none could tell who I was or whence I came."

"Have you that *bulla?*"

"It was taken from me by the pirates who brought me to Rome."

"Can you describe it?"

"Surely. It hung by a gold chain of fine workmanship, and was itself of gold, from which my foster-parents concluded that I must have been free-born, and not the child of a slave. It was about two finger-breadths across, oval rather than round, and somewhat flat, and on the front it bore, engraved in relief, the figure of an armed man on horseback. The boss on his shield was a tiny pearl. On the back were engraved, as I have said, the letters TIB, and on opening the halves of the *bulla* one found within the hollow a braid of hair something less than a span in length, two of the strands being yellow, the third, red. The yellow hair was fine, like a woman's; the red, coarser. The ends of this braid were clipped with bands of gold. Such, *Domina,* was my *bulla.*"

"When was this wreck?"

"Sixteen years ago, or nearly."

"And you have no idea who may be your true parents?"

"None, *Domina.*"

She took from her neck a large cameo, hung on a chain, and passed it silently to the consul, who examined it carefully, from time to time looking at me.

"Turn your side face, Tiberius," he ordered, and I obeyed.

In a moment he handed the jewel back to her, saying:

"It is the same, beyond a doubt."

"Tiberius." Flava addressed me, "have you a

small black mole on your back, on the right shoulder-blade?"

I laughed.

"I am told that I had such a one, yes. But this
man"—I pointed to Pugnax—"removed it with
his sword-point when we fought in the arena last
summer."

"Show me the scar."

Turning my back, I slipped my tunic off, and Flava
inspected the mark of Pugnax' blade.

"You may dress," she told me, and I donned the
tunic again.

"Have you no recollection of anything before
your adoption?" Flava pursued, to which I answered:

"I can vaguely recall a man who spoke kindly to
me, and tied me to a block of wood during a storm.
Also, still vaguely, of being tossed about by the
waters. Nothing else."

"This man—had he red hair like your own?"

"As to that, I cannot say, *Domina*."

Flava, Terentia, and the consul conferred together in an undertone, then Cicero said:

"There can be no doubt. But to make all secure
and legal, a formal adoption—"

"That can wait," Flava interrupted; she was
greatly excited, her bosom heaving with emotion,
her eyes glistening with unshed tears.

Then, to my utter amazement, she rose, flung her arms about me, and kissed me on both cheeks. I was horrified—a patrician woman embracing a slave!

"*Domina!*" I protested, and again: "*Domina!*" Had Fulvia done the like, I would have been disgusted, but neither surprised nor shocked; this woman, though, was a different sort.

But neither Cicero nor Terentia seemed to regard her conduct as out of the way. Flava must have noted my horror, for she drew back, laid both hands on my shoulders, and smiled up at me, asking:

"May not a woman, whatever her station, embrace her own son?"

"Her son?" I repeated, stupidly, and Flava, seeing that I did not understand, said:

"The man whom you remember was my husband, Quintus Cornelius Rufus, and your own father. He was lost at sea, returning from Alexandria to Rome, and it was thought that all on board were lost as well; being in poor health, I had not accompanied him, but remained in the City. Oh, it is beyond question, my Tiberius! The likeness, the red hair, the *bulla,* the mole—how often have I kissed that same mole, when you were a baby!—all join to prove it. Even the legal mind of Cicero, here, admits that the evidence is convincing, that you are my

139

son, Tiberius Cornelius Rufus, whom I mourned as dead." She embraced me again, with greater fervor than before, then held me off at arm's length and stared at me as though to devour me with her eyes. Her features worked, and she seemed about to weep, but with an effort she regained her composure and smiled instead, exclaiming: "The hours that I have mourned for you, Tiberius! The nights when I have lain awake till cock-crow, moistening the pillow with tears for my only son, my baby! You were a darling baby, Tiberius! So sturdy, so bold! How you used to run to your father and me, your little hands up-reaching to us, your sweet voice calling to us! And when you stumbled and fell, you never cried, but picked yourself up, laughing through the tears. Your father used to call you his little soldier."

A flash of recollection came to me.

"I remember those words!" I cried. "It is what he called me as he bound me to the great block of wood, during the storm. *Miles parvulus meus!* I remember!"

And now Flava's tears overflowed, and she strained me to her, openly weeping.

As for me, I was stunned, and I defy any man to receive such news unmoved. Fisher lad, slave, gladiator, patrician—what changes of fortune lay in those four words! I could not grasp it, but stammered out the first thought that came into my head.

"Then . . . then I am kin to Lentulus Sura; he also is of the Cornelian gens."

"Does that please you?" asked Flava. "Do you specially admire him?"

"*Edepol!* Far from it!" I blurted out, and all laughed at my earnestness.

"You will be relieved to learn, then," my mother told me, "that the relationship is remote. So distant, in fact, that it need not worry you." She hugged me again, and this time I returned her embrace. Over her shoulder I caught sight of Pugnax, and had to laugh at the expression on his countenance; Roscius the actor might have taken him for a mask of stupefied amazement, for he stared at me as though I were some strange animal from foreign lands, or some portent or omen in the sky.

"In truth," spoke up Cicero, "I am convinced that you are the son of my old friend, Quintus Rufus. Your face is his, your hair is his, and what you have told us of your history accords with what we know of his departure from this world. In the eyes of Rome you will be his son, though I would strongly advise a legal adoption, to guard against any trouble over the inheritance, when Flava joins her husband. That, however, may rest for the present There is a more immediate matter of which I would speak."

"May I first ask a question, *Domine?*" I inquired, and the consul raised his hand.

"No longer *'Domine,'*" he said. "I am 'Tullius' to the son of my friend."

"Tullius, then." How strangely the word came to my lips! "I am a slave. How can I assume a place in my mother's house?"

"No free-born Roman," he explained, "may be enslaved except for debt or if he voluntarily sell himself into slavery. In theory—in strict law—a *pater familias* may sell a child, but it is doubtful if the courts would sustain such an act, and in any case there is no such question here. And further, I do not believe that your master will long be in a position to maintain property rights in any of his slaves."

"Another thing," I said. "I have been engaged in conspiracy against the State. I see my error— but there it is. I would not have you think I fear to die," I added, hastily, "but it would seem harsh to my mother to regain a son only to have him . . . outlawed."

Cicero waved his hand.

"I understand," he assured me, kindly. "You were misled, and no wonder; Catilina is known for his persuasive tongue. Well. . . ." He thought for a moment, then smiled. "I have it. My chief desire, at the moment, is to force the conspirators to

declare themselves, or, failing that, to secure proof
for a conviction. To-morrow I will ask the Senate
to proclaim a free pardon and a reward for any
who will give confirmation of the plot. It will be a
simple matter to make it retroactive, and thus clear
both you and your friend, whose name I do not
know."

"Pugnax," I said.

"Pugnax. Is he by any chance also of patrician
birth?"

Pugnax grinned and shook his head.

"No, *Domine*," he answered. "I am of Gallia
Transalpina. A slave and naught else, *vae mihi!*
But I rejoice at the good fortune that has descended
on Tiberius."

Cicero turned to my mother.

"Is it your intention, Flava, to claim your son
publicly and at once?"

"In the name of our father Quirinus! What else,
Marcus?"

"As a favor to me, would you not let matters
stand as they are for a short time? Or if that is
not enough inducement, then to aid Rome?"

"Explain yourself."

"I will do so. Here is Tiberius, close to Catilina,
a member of the conspiracy, present at their meetings, privy to all their plans. How could he do
more for the State than by continuing his present

mode of life, and keeping me informed from time to time of what is planned? I am assuming, Tiberius, that you wish to aid Rome?"

It is marvellous what a change is wrought in one's view-point by a change of position! A few hours before, when a slave, I had thought it well to overturn the government, even by armed rebellion; now, a patrician, one of the nobles, I felt myself opposed to the revolt. That is, I think I did; it is hard to look back over a space of years and say just what one thought at a given time, so it may be that I was merely confused in my mind and ready to agree with whatever the consul suggested. At all events, I assured him that I wanted to help the State as best I might. But then a sudden thought struck me.

"You want me to spy on them?"

" 'Spy' is a harsh word," Cicero answered. "Say, rather, to keep me informed of whatever may come to your attention."

But gloss it as he might, it would still be spying, and I liked the idea but little. True, I had spied on them in the beginning, but a slave has no dignity to lose; he may do what a patrician may not, and I was already feeling myself allied to the class of my birth. Cicero must have seen my repugnance, for he said:

"Bear in mind, my Tiberius, that though the task is distasteful, yet it is for Rome."

How I Transferred My Allegiance

I gulped and nodded.

"Very well, Tullius," I told him, using his name to bolster up my resolution, "I will do it."

"Good lad!" he approved, but even as he spoke another idea flashed across my mind, and with a groan I buried my face in my hands and dropped into a chair.

"My master!" I said.

"What of him?"

"This! He has been a good master to me. He took me from Dumnorix' school, he has treated me with kindness—and I shall be betraying him. Surely the Fates have cast me for the part of villain in the drama of life! First Rome, then my master—to whom shall I next be false?"

Sick at heart, I wept aloud. Do you blame me? Sell yourself into slavery, find yourself driven to choose between the death of your benefactor and your own death, steel yourself to die in agony and disgrace—then suddenly find yourself not only free and safe, but lifted to noble rank, and a friend of the greatest man in all the State. Then have him show that your duty is to betray to shame and death one who has been kind to you. If your nerves withstand the shock they are stouter than mine—and I was for two years a gladiator.

But Cicero understood. Rising, he stepped to where I sat, and laid his hand on my shoulder.

"Be comforted, my Tiberius," he said. "I can feel for you, but consider what it means if this revolt succeeds. You have not seen, as I have, the gutters of Rome running with the blood of her best —not richest, but best—citizens. You have not seen orators, patriots, statesmen, slaughtered like bullocks at the nod of a savage tyrant; the Treasury looted, the offices in the hands of Rome's vilest, and innocent men accused before the courts of parricide, that most unthinkable crime against Gods and men, merely that some greedy tool of the conqueror may enjoy in peace their inheritance. Before all the Gods, Tiberius, I swear to you that should the spirit of Sulla return in the body of Catilina, I, the Roman consul, would with my own hand slay myself rather than live again through such a time of blood and lust and terror as that through which I lived at your age. Tiberius, think! Be warned in time. Conceive what it means to let loose on Rome the slaves of the City, the scum of the Subura, the off-scourings of the rural slave-prisons. You have lived among gladiators, you know their savagery, their lusts—are they men to be loosed on the women of Rome? Can you believe that any restraint will hold them back? And can you think of any worse horror than for them to sweep, free from all restraint, through the homes of the City? *Di bene vortant!* The Gods forbid! Yet these are the men whom Catilina plans to loose on Rome—it were kinder to unleash a pack of starving wolves!

"And as for your feelings, I can understand and appreciate them; gratitude is too rare an emotion to be scorned, and I have too recently benefited by it to despise it. But which is your duty—to feed your own sense of gratitude, or to avert, by any means in your power, the dreadful tide of blood and fire and slaughter that Catilina plans for the City that gave him birth? Look at your mother, Flava, who in joy of spirit and agony of body gave you life; look at my daughter Tullia; if there is perchance some woman on whom your affections are placed, think of her. Then think, call up to your mind the picture of these and hundreds more, with hair unbound and garments torn and stained, fleeing in terror from the bloody hands of Dumnorix' men. Son of my friend, you have my sympathy—but you are a Roman, and duty calls!"

Who could resist such a man? I remembered what he was doing for the State, remembered that he went in daily—nay, hourly—peril of his life, that for him the daggers of assassins were sharpened, that on him the hatred of the nobles was poured; and that through this hate, these perils, he walked unmoved of soul. And men called him a coward! *Per Deos Immortales!* The Gods grant that in such case I too might show such courage!

I rose and extended my hand. He pressed it firmly, then turned to my mother.

"Flava," he asked, "do you consent that your son remain a slave yet a few weeks longer?"

"I too am a Roman, Marcus," she answered, simply, and he smiled.

"It is agreed, then, that you are to act as though this night had never been, and are to find means to let me know what further is planned." He turned to my friend. "Pugnax," he asked, "how is it with you?"

"Where Tiberius goes, I go," answered Pugnax, and the consul, nodding, said:

"I thought as much. Then it is arranged. And now you had best depart; my friends will be here soon, and it will save question and answer if you are away."

It was too late, though, for even as Pugnax and I were preparing to leave, Gaius Caesar was announced, and hot at his heels came Quintus Cicero and Lucius Flaccus, with Cato no more than a minute behind them. Explanations followed, and Cato said:

"How of these slaves, my Tullius? They are deep in the conspiracy, by their own showing. Are they not food for the cross?"

"I have promised them immunity," the consul replied. "I can scarcely give the word to crucify men who have just saved my life."

"*Per Martes*, no!" exclaimed Flaccus.

"You were always too soft-hearted, Tullius," Cato grumbled. "There can be no compromise with duty, and they are self-confessed traitors against the State."

"You must let me have my own way in this, my friend," the consul insisted, smiling. "I am not so stern in my conception of duty as you are. All Rome knows that Cato is no temporizer, but we weaker men must sometimes bow to circumstance." He glanced across at Caesar as he spoke, and I could swear I saw his eyelid flicker—and I know that the ghost of a smile played for an instant on Caesar's lips.

Cato grumbled some further remonstrance, then subsided, and Quintus Cicero spoke.

"Get you to bed, Marcus," he told his brother. "We will watch and see that you are not disturbed. Tell your *janitor* to refuse admittance to Vargunteius and Cornelius—men of good family turned dagger-men!—and should they get in by guile or force—well, we will take care of them. Eh, Gaius?"

Caesar nodded silently, and I felt a pang of sorrow for the two assassins, should they gain entrance; Caesar later proved himself the greatest general and statesman of all time, but then I merely knew him as the foremost athlete and swordsman in Rome. I had observed him looking intently at me, and I found out later that he recognized me at once for the son of Quintus Rufus; there was little that escaped his piercing eye, his giant brain. But Caesar had a gift for silence, and he exercised it now.

Pugnax and I took our departure, the consul restoring our daggers and giving us a torch as we left.

"It is not well to walk the streets unarmed and in darkness," he said. "Good-night, my Romans."

Once outside, Pugnax drew a deep breath and turned to me.

"Of all the astounding luck!" he exclaimed. "*Domine,* Fortuna was in—"

I caught him a blow of my fist alongside the head and sent him reeling into the gutter.

"You dare to call me '*Domine!*'" I said. "Once and for all, I am 'Tiberius' to you. '*Domine,*' indeed!"

He rubbed his ear ruefully.

"But you are a patrician, and I a slave. It is not fitting—"

"Fitting or not, you heard me," I interrupted. "You will understand, here and now, that I am 'Tiberius' to you. Forget it, and we cease to be friends."

"Oh, as you say," he assented. He rubbed his ear again. *"Edepol,* your fist has grown no softer since we left the school! But, my Tiberius, Fortuna was in a generous mood when she cast your horoscope."

"You are not envious?" I deprecated. "It was not my doing."

"Envious! For what do you take me? No, I rejoice in your good fortune. But I cannot help wishing that some few crumbs from such a feast might fall my way."

I caught his hand and examined it.

"I see no nail-holes in your palm," I told him, and he laughed. "Seriously, though," I went on, "I think some few crumbs will be yours. Apart from the fact that we have escaped the cross, did you not hear what the consul said when he bade us good-night?"

"What do you mean?"

"He said, 'Good-night, my Romans.'"

Pugnax halted in his tracks and grasped my arm.

"Did he mean . . . well, what do you think . . . do you think he meant. . . ."

"I do," was my reply. "I think he meant precisely that. And if he did not, I do. Let us live through this affair, let me but come to my patrimony, and you are a free man, my Pugnax. That much I promise you. And if the consul and I be-

tween us can bring it about—and it will be strange
if we cannot—you shall be a Roman citizen."

"*Mehercle!*" he sighed. "I can scarce credit it.
A Roman citizen! Yes, Tiberius, certain crumbs
are falling my way . . . a citizen of Rome!"

CHAPTER VII

Of the First Oration; and the Fight at the Porta Carmentalis

IT was not far from dawn when I reached home, so rousing one of the slaves and bidding him call me at an early hour, I stretched out on my couch for a little rest. Catilina—I could no longer think of him as my master—had ordered me to be early at the home of Metellus, but I could snatch an hour or two of sleep before setting out.

As in the gray light before sunrise I led my men along the empty streets of the Palatine I shivered from time to time. I drew my cloak tighter about me, telling myself that it was the chill air which made gooseflesh on my arms and back, but within my heart I knew that this was not wholly true. It was, to be sure, a brisk, snappy November dawn, crisp and clear, but there was more to it than that; I have always been inclined to shiver when going into danger, and the Gods knew well I was in peril now. Should any of Cicero's slaves have mentioned that Tiberius the Red was at the house—! Well, I was armed, and could make a fight, at least; further, I comforted myself with the thought that my uneasiness always left me when the fighting began.

Reaching Metellus' home, I was admitted, going to the dining-room, where I found Catilina eating his breakfast of bread and cheese and wine in company with the praetor. They greeted me pleasantly enough, asked if I had breakfasted, and on learning that I had not, they ordered in food for me, which I ate standing. By the time they had finished, the sun was fully up, and Metellus excused himself, saying that he had some cases coming before him that morning, and must be off to the courts. I followed Catilina to the *atrium,* where he showed an unusual restlessness, pacing tiger-like up and down, and stopping often to examine the *clepsydra.*

At length there came a knocking at the street door, and he stopped to listen; it may perhaps be understood that I was no less tense than he was, though I dared not show it. A slave entered, announcing two gentlemen, and prompt on his heels came Vargunteius and Cornelius, white-lipped and shaking. Catilina waited until the slave had withdrawn, then hurried to the dagger-men.

"Well?" he demanded. "Well? Is it done?"

"We are betrayed," Vargunteius stammered, and Cornelius echoed: "Betrayed!"

"Betrayed!" stormed Catilina. "Speak, man, speak! Tell your story."

"There is naught to tell," answered Vargunteius; and Cornelius, who seemed bereft of ideas of his own, parroted, "Naught!"

"We went to the consul's house, as agreed," Vargunteius explained. "And were refused admittance." About here I set my teeth and laid hand on my sword-hilt; if trouble was coming, now was the time.

"Was no reason given?" Catilina demanded, and the two, shaking their heads, replied together:

"None."

"*Per Deos Immortales!*" swore Catilina. "Was Cicero receiving?"

"He was. We saw others enter and leave. But we were denied admittance."

"And no reason given? Incredible!"

"No reason given. The *janitor* merely said that the consul had given him our names, with orders not to admit us. No more than that."

I began to breathe more freely.

"*Per Martes!*" Catilina bit his lip till the blood ran down his chin, whereat he wiped it impatiently with his kerchief. "It is plain; someone in our counsels has betrayed us . . . Pluto seize him! But who? Who?"

The others shrugged, and Catilina whirled on me.

"Tiberius," he demanded, savagely. "have you knowledge of this?"

"I, *Domine?*" I answered, looking as surprised and innocent as possible. "No, *Domine*, by Pluto, no. How should I have?" I believe the Gods will forgive the lie, seeing in what cause it was told. Catilina's face softened.

"I did not mean that you had betrayed us," he said. "I know you would not do such a thing." (*Edepol,* that hurt!) "But I thought you might have some suspicion of the traitor."

"No, *Domine*," I told him, steadily. "Would that I had!" And I gripped my sword-hilt.

"It might be Volturcius," Cornelius suggested, and Catilina nodded.

"In truth, yes," he agreed. "Or any of half a dozen others. Statilius is a weak sister, and Lentulus Sura is frightened nearly to death by the portents. Coeparius, too . . . well, we cannot decide it now." He turned again to me. "Tiberius, do you go to all our people, and bid them meet to-night at Laeca's. The usual time. Go!"

"Yes, *Domine*." Saluting, I departed on my errand—and drew the first free breath I had taken for some hours past.

I was not, however, altogether easy in mind. I did not know when some whisper might get back to Catilina, what slave might rouse suspicion by a casual remark as to the hour of my return the night before, or who might have seen Pugnax and me going or coming on our errand to Cicero's. I have ever been calm and collected when actually fighting, but I have never been able to conquer the nervousness that assails me while waiting for the fight to start. But after all, nothing untoward happened, and we met according to custom, in the house in the Street of the Scythe-Makers, shortly after dark.

The meeting was a stormy one. Accusations and recriminations flew thick and stinging as hail, and Cethegus and Vargunteius fell into a quarrel, drew their daggers, and only with difficulty were separated by the rest of us. The brawl flared up when Cethegus accused Vargunteius of cowardice, and the latter gave him the lie direct. I could hardly blame him, for whatever may have been Vargunteius' faults, assuredly he was no poltroon. Laeca and Lentulus Sura quarreled, also, the former elegantly calling Lentulus "a quavering bag of guts," and here too daggers were drawn; Lentulus might safely be faulted for lack of courage, but he violently resented an allusion to his fat. And a few hot words passed between Sempronia and Curius, Fulvia supporting her lover in language which would have shocked my old acquaintances Gaza and Sportella. There was other wrangling, as well, so that all in all it was a vivacious evening, and the efforts of the cooler-headed were taxed to prevent bloodshed.

At length some measure of peace was secured, and for the time being the gates of Janus were closed. Catilina rose to address the assembly.

"It has been agreed," he said, "that I should join the army and direct their actions, while you others conduct affairs within the City. This seems to me wise, but it is plain from Cicero's refusal to admit our two friends to his house, this morning, that to say the least, he suspects us. Indeed, he has publicly said as much, and further, he claims to have definite knowledge of our plans. His action in occupying Praeneste ahead of Manlius lends support to the claim, from which I have thought that we had among us a traitor who was keeping him informed of our doings.

"But on considering the matter, I believe I may be mistaken. Think! If he had any certain knowledge, would he hesitate to move against us? Would the opposition of the nobles restrain him, when his own life is in peril? He claims that his desire is to force us to declare ourselves, that he may be held blameless when he condemns Roman citizens to death; does that seem to you probable? True, he appears—note that I say *appears*—to have some knowledge of our plans, our actions, but is that not a clever guess rather than certainty? Undoubtedly he knows that something is in the wind, but is not his apparent knowledge a shrewd guess? We all know that the consul—I speak of Cicero rather than his colleague Antonius—we all know that Cicero— Pluto seize him!—is one of the cleverest, shrewdest men in Rome, and I would not place it beyond him to be guessing, perhaps from some vague hints, at all that he has said; I cannot believe that if he had actual knowledge he would remain idle.

"Now, he has called a meeting of the Senate for to-morrow, in the Temple of Jupiter Stator, and I am supposed to attend. Would it not give rise to talk should I absent myself? Should I be seen leaving the City and taking the road to Faesulae, would it not be held as confirmation of all that Cicero has told the Senate? It is my opinion that it would, and I feel that to disarm suspicion I should be present to-morrow; after the meeting I can perhaps depart from the City as though going on business, without giving rise to talk. Let me hear your views."

As ever, there was a hot debate, some saying one thing and some another, and listening, I thought to myself that there was a potent cause for failure in the divided opinions of the conspirators. I may be wrong, but it does not seem to me that any great cause can be truly guided by even the wisest group; there should be one strong man at the head, to give orders for the others to follow. Some fifteen years later it was my fortune to be one of Gaius Caesar's

military tribunes during the Civil War, and Jove
see me! there was no disputing or quarreling in his
command! Caesar gave orders, and we obeyed.

But in the end the others came around to Catilina's view, it was decided that he should attend the
meeting of the Senate on the morrow, and we took
our leave of Marcus Laeca. At Metellus' home,
Catilina bade me good-night, instructing me to report there early the following morning, and I went
home, my mind somewhat relieved; it was evident
that no one had betrayed my visit to the consul.

The next day was the sixth before the Ides of
November,* a day that I shall never forget, though
I live past the century mark. I have seen many an
eventful day, but none surpasses this in my recollection, not even that one when at Pharsalus the flower
of Rome, under command of Pompeius Magnus,
broke and fled in utter rout before the veterans of
the great Iulius, nor that other when the fleet of
Antonius, deserted by Cleopatra, was shattered and
smashed by the onslaught of Octavius Caesar.

We were early at the Temple of Jupiter, on the
Palatine, and I observed an unusual number of
soldiers drawn up both without and within the
Senate chamber, from which I concluded that Cicero
was taking precautions against such an attack as,
nineteen years later, was fatal to the greatest Roman

* November 8.

who ever lived or shall live. Entering the building, Catilina passed at once into the Senate chamber, while I, taking my post outside the door, saw that though most of the senators were still absent, the consul sat grim and silent in his curule chair, his purple-bordered toga drawn close about his still figure. As the others drifted in by ones and twos and in groups he responded only by a nod to their greetings, but when all were in their places he got to his feet, adjusted the folds of his toga, and drew a deep breath. He seemed to be struggling with some powerful emotion, then as all eyes were turned on him, as all present listened eagerly, he mastered himself and spoke. He did not begin with the usual salutation of *"Patres Conscripti,"* but in tones vibrant with passion he broke at once into that terrible invective which will live as long as the Roman tongue endures, the First Oration Against Catilina.

"How far, then, oh Catilina, will you abuse our patience? How much longer will that madness of yours insult us? To what limit will that unbridled audacity of yours hurl itself about? Has neither the nightly guard on the Palatine, nor the watch placed over the City, nor the alarm of the people, nor the union of all good men, nor this most securely guarded meeting-place for the Senate, nor the faces of these men here present—has none of these things had any effect on you? Do you not realize that your plans lie open in the sight of all? Do you not see that your conspiracy is held powerless by the knowledge of all these men? Whom among us do you believe ignorant of what you did last night and the night before, of where you were, of those whom you called together, of what plans you made?

"Oh, shame on the age and on its morals! The Senate knows these things, the consul sees them— yet this man lives! Lives? Aye, he even comes into the Senate, shares in the public debates, and meanwhile notes and marks off for death each one among us. And we, brave men! we think that we have done our duty by the State if we ourselves avoid his rage and his weapons! Catilina, the consul should long since have condemned you to death, should long since have brought down upon your head the destruction which you so long have planned for us all!"

It is not my intention to quote the whole of this tremendous speech; those who care to read it may find it in any of the book-shops of the Argiletum— but, alas, they will not find the resonant, sonorous voice and the impressive manner of the great orator; these live only in the memories of the fortunate ones who heard him. Suffice it to say that the consul laid bare all the plans of the conspirators, told of the meeting at Laeca's, of Manlius' rising, and of the plot for his own assassination and how it was frus-

trated. He censured the men who by their mild-
ness and disbelief had encouraged the conspiracy,
besought them to be warned in time, promised that
the vigilance of the consuls would continue, and ad-
jured Catilina to take himself and his vile associates
out of the City. And he closed with a magnificent
prayer to Jupiter Stator, in whose temple we were,
that He would protect the State against these infamous men, banded together in crime, and would
visit upon them, in this world and the next, the
punishment they deserved.

As the consul spoke, one after another of the
senators who sat near Catilina rose and moved
away, until he sat isolated, alone, a marked man.
The praetor at whose house he was staying, Marcus
Metellus, had taken a seat at Catilina's elbow, but
he was the first to move, a look of horror and contempt upon his face. Marcus Cato followed him
at once, then in a moment Gaius Caesar changed
his place, and with him went Lucius Flaccus. Then
Decimus Silanus, the consul-elect, went to a distant
seat, and after him Quintus Sanga, and others followed, until before the speech was half done there
was no one within five paces of Catilina.

Catilina's features wore first, as the consul began,
a look of consternation; then, as the tide of invective rose and swelled, this was replaced by an
expression of despair; and finally, regaining his com-

posure, he put on a mask of confidence. When at length Cicero ended and took his seat, Catilina rose to address the Conscript Fathers. But he was greeted by a howl of execration and abuse, and many, leaping from their seats, shook their fists at him in rage, so that the whole Senate chamber was in an uproar. Furious, he glared about, waiting to make himself heard, but each time he opened his mouth to speak, the storm broke out afresh. I saw the veins in his neck and temples swell, his face became congested and purple, and he trembled from head to foot with anger, until at last he could no longer control himself, but stamped his foot, shook both fists at the storming crowd, and with a bellowed curse turned and rushed from the Temple. As in duty bound, I followed him through the streets to his own home.

Once within the *atrium,* Catilina flung himself into a chair, where for some minutes he rested, silent and brooding. Then straightening up, he broke into a stream of cursing. He cursed Cicero, the Senate, and Rome; he cursed the patricians, the equestrians, the plebeians, and the slaves; he cursed Vargunteius and Cornelius for cowards, Fulvia for a loose-tongued boaster, and the unknown spy who had betrayed the conspiracy. And finally—here I moved inconspicuously from his immediate neighborhood —he bestowed one last crackling curse upon Jupiter

Stator and the Hearth of Vesta! However, no crashing thunderbolt marked the wrath of the Gods at this blasphemy, and, his fury expended, Catilina fell silent once more.

Presently he roused himself.

"Ha, Tiberius!" he said. "You there?"

"Yes, *Domine*," I replied. "As ever, when you want me."

"You are a good lad," he acknowledged. *"Per Martes!* Would that everyone were as faithful to me! That mangy hound of a consul would not have said what he did to-day. You heard him?"

"Yes, *Domine*."

"Yes, of course; you were there. And you saw how the Senate treated me?"

"Yes, *Domine*."

"Per Deos Immortales! I will have their lives for it! One of the Sergian gens to be scorned and hooted down at the bidding of an upstart equestrian, a new man! May his teeth rot from his jaw, his flesh from his bones, and may his soul be pursued forever through the realms of Dis by harpies! As Mars looks down upon me, I will have revenge— by our sire Quirinus I swear it!" With an effort he calmed himself. "Enough of that," he said. "Tiberius, there is no longer any reason to stay within the City. To-night I ride to join Manlius; you will accompany me."

"Yes, *Domine*," I acknowledged the order. I did not like it much, however; I had no desire to leave Rome just then, and, further, I craved to be set free from attendance on Catilina. It was no easy task that Cicero had given me—to spy on a man who had treated me well, to betray one who trusted me, to listen to words of praise for my constancy, and at the same time to know myself for a slimy traitor. I resolved that, Rome or no Rome, I would free myself as soon as possible; there are limits to what a man can bear. I would perhaps have felt better had I known how soon my release was to come, but the Gods deny us foreknowledge of Their plans.

"It may be that the consul will have guards at the Porta Flumentana to stop us," Catilina went on, "so we will leave by the Porta Carmentalis, where the centurion on guard is one of our men, and we will cross Tiber at the Island, by the Pons Fabricius and the Pons Cestius. Then into the Via Aurelia, through Janiculum, and so to Etruria. Bid Glaucus and Lucipor have horses—four of them—at the junction of the Via Nova and the Vicus Tuscus. We will meet them at midnight—I have much to do in the meantime—and the four of us will go."

"Only four, *Domine?* Not the whole body-guard?"

"Two only, besides ourselves. Now be about it,

and see that the horses are good ones. And send
my secretary to me as you go; I have letters to
write."

"Yes, *Domine.*" And saluting, I retired.

That was a busy day for Catilina, and but little
less so for me. He kept his secretary busy writing
from dictation, and sent me and three other slaves
scurrying hither and thither with letters. Everywhere I went I saw knots of people gathered in the
Forum and in the streets, and one such group—
rabble, they were, not patricians—hissed me as I
passed. I paid no attention to that, but when I was
some ten paces beyond them a stone buzzed past my
ear. At that my temper flared up, and I whirled
and walked quickly back toward them, drawing my
dagger as I went. But they separated in flight,
and it would have been foolish to pursue.

One of Catilina's letters was to Quintus Curius,
but I did not find him at home. His major-domo
told me that he had gone to Fulvia's, whither I went
at once, to find that he had not yet arrived. I
decided to leave the letter with Pugnax, and so
found an opportunity of talking with my friend, of
telling him what Catilina was about to do.

"So you are going to Etruria, to the army?" said
Pugnax.

"Needs must," I answered. "I have orders to

167

watch Catilina and to keep Cicero informed, as
you very well know."

"And how do you propose to do that last? Are
you taking a flock of trained pigeons?" Pugnax
was at times a trifle sarcastic.

I laughed.

"Hardly," I replied. "Conceal them in the folds
of my tunic? But I shall find means to get word
back. Is Polla about?"

"I will find her." And he went in search.

Presently the two returned, and I gave my sister
a brief account of what I was about to do. She
was no little worried at the prospect of my being
with the army, and gave me an amulet to protect
me from danger.

"I bought it to-day," she told me. "I meant it for
Pugnax," she added, naïvely, "but your peril is
greater. And I can get him another."

The charm was a bronze medal, bearing on one
side the words: *"Vesta me custodiet,"* and on the
other a profile of the Goddess. I have little faith
in such things, but at least they can do no harm,
and—who knows?—they may help. Indeed, within
twelve hours this very amulet was of great benefit
to me, and it may be that Vesta took that way of
answering my sister's prayer; we cannot know for
certain the purposes of the Gods. At all events, I
allowed Polla to hang the charm about my neck

by a leather thong, while Pugnax, watching, pretended jealousy.

"Thus goes it ever," he grumbled. "A maid favors one man till a handsomer comes along. Plague on your good-looking face, Tiberius! I did think, though, that Polla would be true to me."

She flew to him, flinging her arms about his neck and kissing him.

"I do love you, my Pugnax, I do!" she protested. "But Tiberius is my brother, and he is going into danger."

"Oh, very well, very well!" he told her. "Give him my amulet, by all means. Give it to him, do. Is there anything else of mine you would like him to have? My sword? My dagger? It is a good dagger; shall I give it to him, and go unarmed?" Then, seeing that she was inclined to take him seriously, and was on the verge of tears, he laughed and kissed her. Pouting, she turned away.

"You always tease me," she said. "You're horrid! I hate you! No, go away; I don't love you when you tease; I won't kiss you again. No, go away!"

Much as I enjoyed watching the lovers amuse themselves with their pretence of quarreling, it was time to go, so I said good-bye to Polla and motioned Pugnax to accompany me to the door. There, clasping his hand, I said:

"The Gods willing, we shall meet soon. Meanwhile, I leave her in your charge."

His honest, homely face glowed with fervor as he gripped my hand, replying:

"With my life. Farewell."

I went my way, knowing that my sister would be as safe through the coming troubles as any woman could be; if necessary, Pugnax would slay her himself to save her from a worse fate.

Returning home, I made sure that Glaucus and Lucipor selected the best four of all the horses in our stables, and ordered them to have the animals bridled and waiting at the appointed place a half hour before midnight; Catilina was to dine and spend the evening at Cethegus' house, discussing plans, and we would go from there to the rendezvous.

Accordingly, about the tenth hour we set out, and immediately upon our arrival at Cethegus', where the others were already waiting, we went to the dining-room. There were present, besides the host and Catilina, Lentulus Sura, Curius, Capito, Statilius, Coeparius, Sempronia, and Fulvia, so the couches were just filled; of course, being a slave, I remained standing. It is significant of the position of Sempronia and Fulvia that they did not occupy chairs, but reclined like the men.

The food was excellent, plentiful, and well

cooked, and I made a good meal on what was handed to me. The wine, too, was the best Falernian, and by the time the wreaths were brought in all but Catilina, Sempronia, and I were drinking it undiluted, with the natural result that we were the only ones who did not become drunk. The others remonstrated when the two insisted that their wine be watered, but Catilina pointed out that he had a hard ride before him, and they yielded; Sempronia gave no reason, but merely insisted, and carried her point. At length it came time to leave, and Catilina rose from his couch, steady as a rock, cold as the white peak of Soracte. He looked the others over, then, contemptuously:

"Bah!" he snorted. "A fine lot they are! Circe's magic potions would be wasted on them."

He spoke the truth; they were a septet of swine. Cethegus was asleep, snoring like a hog; Curius also slept, lying on his back, Fulvia's head pillowed on his shoulder, she hiccoughing in her sleep; Coeparius had long since rolled from his couch to the floor, where he grunted and snorted, half sitting, half reclining, his chaplet awry, an empty goblet clutched in his hand; Lentulus Sura was chewing the rose petals of his wreath and proclaiming that he was a faun—and a less faun-like figure I never saw!—while Capito and Statilius were busily emptying goblets on each other's heads and laughing like maniacs. And one and all were stained and splashed with wine. Save Catilina and myself, Sempronia was the only sober one there, and she rose as we prepared to go, accompanying us to the door.

"They are indeed a foolish lot, my Sergius," she said, as I laid the cloak about his shoulders and buckled on his sword-belt. "Do you not fear for our enterprise, with such as these aiding us?"

He gave her a look full of meaning, then:

"It is too late now," he said, gloomily. "We are fully committed. Another time—but there may be no other time."

"Sergius," she asked, "what of my husband?"

"Decimus Brutus? He had his chance to join us, and refused."

"I do not mean that," replied she. "But . . . but . . . is he to be . . . proscribed?"

"Do you so desire?"

Sempronia looked down, twisting her fingers together like an embarrassed peasant maid.

"No," she answered, in a small voice. "No."

"You love him?" Catilina seemed surprised.

"I do not love him. But . . . he has been good to me. I would not have him. . . ."

"Be content, Sempronia. He shall be spared. And now farewell."

She held out her hand, saying:

"The Gods be with you, Sergius."

SHE HELD OUT HER HAND, SAYING: "THE GODS BE
WITH YOU, SERGIUS."

He grasped it, then bent and kissed her.

"And with you, Sempronia. Farewell. **Come, Tiberius.**"

And the door shut her from our sight.

Once outside, Catilina laughed shortly.

"Women are strange things, my Tiberius," he said. "She and Decimus have not been on good terms for years, his death would enrich her and set her free—and she will not have him slain! They are beyond my understanding." Well, I thought I could see how some remnants of tenderness might prompt her reluctance, but it would have been futile to say so, and I merely agreed as we set out for our journey.

The night was clear and sharp, with above us a rich blue sky glittering with stars so close that it seemed as though one might touch them from the roof-tops. Looking westward along the dark and blank-walled street, I saw a half moon swinging low to the horizon, and on the other hand the Belt of the Hunter hung poised in the east, barely above the roofs. The air stung in our nostrils, keen and pleasant after the reek of wine and the heavy perfume of roses, so that we drew deep breaths as we strode quickly through the deserted streets and down the slope toward the waiting horses. Off toward the Forum Boarium we could hear the rumble of carts and the lowing of cattle, and we could see the glare of lights, but on the Palatine all was dark and still save for the thump of our boots on the pavement and the glow of the torch I carried.

In a few minutes we were down the slope and at the foot of the hill, where, at the appointed place, we found Glaucus and Lucipor with the horses. Giving the men a word of praise, Catilina mounted, we three following suit, and we pressed at a fast walk through the Velabrum and the Forum Boarium. This last was a scene of utmost confusion, for, no teaming being allowed in the City during the day, the country folk must bring in their produce by night, dispose of it to the store-keepers, and be outside the wall by dawn. At least, that was the law, though as a matter of fact, if they were away by noon no trouble was raised; the Forum Boarium being close by the wall, they did not interfere with the City traffic. So what with the tossing lights, the rumble of wheels, the clatter of hoofs on the cobbles, the lowing of cattle and grunting of hogs, as well as the shouts and oaths of the farmers, it is difficult to imagine a wilder spectacle.

Nor was there lacking humor of a boisterous kind, and for all our haste we stopped to laugh at one ridiculous incident. Two carts, going in opposite directions, locked wheels, and both drivers being obstinate, neither would back up, but with curses at each other they lashed their horses furiously. As a result, the wheel was stripped from one cart, which promptly fell over on its side, spilling out a dozen or so half-grown pigs. Squealing madly, these scampered in all directions, upsetting several people, and one of them bounced from the hind legs of a bull calf which a farmer was leading. The calf went into a panic, jerked loose from its owner, and head down, charged the nearest person. This happened to be a stout farmer who at the moment was leaning over to lace his boot, and the calf, taking him full in the rear, sent him rolling a good twenty feet, then continued on across the Forum, scattering people right and left. We did not wait to see the end of the episode, but pushed on, all four of us rocking on our horses with mirth.

Skirting the foot of the Capitoline, we came to the Porta Carmentalis, where a soldier emerged from the guard-room in response to Catilina's summons.

"Open!" said Catilina. "I must take the road."

But instead of complying, the man drew closer, peering up into Catilina's face.

"Are you not Lucius Sergius Catilina?" he asked.

"I am," was the reply. "What of it? Open the gate."

The man shook his head.

"I was on duty at the Temple of Jupiter Stator this morning," he answered. "And heard the consul denounce you. I will not open the gate for a traitor."

"Fool!" exploded Catilina. "If you heard Cicero's speech you heard him say that I was free to leave the City, that I was free to join Manlius—nay, that he desired me to depart. Wherefore open and let me go. Or summon Aulus Scaevola, your centurion; he knows me, and will give the order to open."

But the soldier was one of those well-intentioned, brainless, honest men who by their stubbornness at times make more trouble than deliberately wicked ones; in a lower sphere, he was such another as Marcus Cato, whom we all respected, and whom we all found, at times, a dreadful nuisance.

"Scaevola is absent," he replied. "Marcus Rapum, the decurion, takes his place. And you do not pass to-night."

For some time Catilina argued with him, trying to persuade him, and even offered him a gold piece, but to no avail; the soldier merely reiterated his refusal. I had seen from the first what might be expected—the flat, stupid countenance told clearly enough that there was no brain behind it—and I had been gradually edging my horse nearer and nearer to the guard. At length I flung myself bodily on the man, pinning his arms to his sides and bearing him to the ground.

"Open and ride!" I shouted. "Quick! Quick!"

Instantly Glaucus and Lucipor were off their horses and tearing at the bar of the gate, while the soldier and I rolled struggling back and forth, and my horse stamped and snorted about, threatening to crush us both. The soldier was a strong man, and though he could not draw his sword he managed to get one arm free and snatched the dagger from my belt, driving it downward at my bosom. The point struck Polla's amulet, glanced off, and raked my ribs instead of piercing my heart, and before he could strike again I drove my knee into his stomach, knocking him breathless. And now men were running from the guard-room, shouting, and now Catilina was through the gate, Glaucus and Lucipor, mounted again, close at his heels. Thrusting the soldier from me, I leaped to my feet and ran for my horse, but he dodged, and so delayed me that just as I grasped the bridle a dozen hands seized me, held fast, and I was disarmed. It was useless to resist, and the soldiers dragged me into the guard-room, where they bound my hands behind me and discussed what was to be done.

The decurion in charge, being roused from slumber in an inner room, listened to what I had to say, then turned to the man whom I had attacked. He told his tale, and wound up:

"I am for despatching him forthwith. He came with Catilina, and he made it possible for the traitor to escape. A sword-thrust is the answer to the problem."

"I am under protection of the consul," I spoke up. "Slay me, and you will greet to-morrow's sun from a cross on the Esquiline."

"Brave words!" sneered another. "What do they mean? Nothing! Is it possible that a man under the protection of the consul would be riding in Catilina's train? A likely story!"

"He may be a spy of Cicero's," was the suggestion from still another of the group.

"What if he is?" demanded the last speaker. "I am with Sextus; settle the matter here and now; Tiber is at hand to receive his carcass. See his pierced ears! What is a slave more or less? Let Tiber have him."

But the decurion shook his head.

"This is no common slave," he told them. "I have seen that red thatch too often in the arena to mistake it; this is Tiberius the gladiator, foremost *retiarius* of Dumnorix' school." He addressed me. "Under which consul are you—Antonius or Cicero?"

"Cicero," I responded, and the decurion smiled.

"The Gods be with you," he said. "Well, so be

it; you have appealed to the consul; by the consul you shall be judged. Tie his feet also, and let him wait for dawn. If he has lied, I would not give a *sestertius* for his chances when he comes face to face with Marcus Tullius. See that he does not escape; it may be that the Esquiline shall bear a cross after all, even if it be not mine."

My ankles were lashed together, a coarse cloth was plastered over my wound to stop the bleeding, and I was rolled into a corner to wait for sunrise. The man I had attacked seized the opportunity to give me a couple of surreptitious kicks in the ribs, but it would not do to let him see that they hurt, so I merely sneered at him, and with an oath he joined the others in the dice game which we had interrupted.

CHAPTER VIII

Of the Second Oration; and the Affair at the Mulvian Bridge

WHEN morning came, two soldiers were detailed to take me to Cicero, and my feet were unbound that I might walk, though my hands were still tied. Back we went over the route I had traversed some hours before, and presented ourselves to the consul as he was receiving his clients. Of course, I was at once freed, but Cicero commended the soldiers for their vigilance and gave them a handful of *denarii* to reward their zeal, so they left the house in good spirits, though somewhat disappointed at not seeing me crucified. When they had gone, the consul bade me wait until he had despatched his business—it took about an hour— and at length he turned to me.

"I thought I told you to remain with Catilina and keep watch over him," he said, sternly. "Is this your obedience, this your fidelity to Rome?"

"So you did, *Domine*—"

"Tullius," he corrected me.

"I ask pardon. Tullius. It is hard to rid myself of custom. But it was no fault of mine that we were separated." I told what had occurred, and the consul admitted that I was not to blame. "I can easily rejoin him," I pointed out. "Shall I do so?"

But the consul shook his head.

"No," he said, after a moment's thought. "No, you can be more useful to me in the City. Continue to live in Catilina's home, and report to me anything you may consider of importance."

I bowed and withdrew, determined to do all in my power to aid the consul; I had no such affection for the other conspirators as I owned for Catilina, and I felt—though perhaps without justification—that his flight from the City had in some way freed me from that obligation.

That afternoon, hearing that Cicero was to address the people, I made my way to the Comitium, and being early I was able to find a place near the Rostra. Not only was the open plaza crowded with people, but the housetops were packed as well, something that invariably happened when Cicero spoke, for we Romans have always loved oratory, and he was everywhere acknowledged the greatest of our speakers, greater even than his famous rival and friend, Hortensius. I knew that I would be in some danger if recognized, but accepted the risk for the sake of hearing Cicero; fortunately, however, no one paid any attention to me, all being intent on the speaker's words. But though I enjoyed listening to the admirably turned phrases and musical voice, I learned nothing new; the speech was merely a description of what had happened, and was intended both to familiarize the people with the steps taken by the consul to break up the plot, and to arouse the Romans to their peril. This was accomplished to perfection, and when the speech was finished I heard on all sides the most extravagant praises of the speaker; he was not only lauded as the foremost orator of all time, greater even than the Grecian Demosthenes, but was hailed without reserve as the savior of Rome. It is impossible to exaggerate the response which he invariably secured, not only from the emotional crowd, but from the intellectual class as well.

On the following day the Senate passed the edict which the consul had promised Pugnax and me, and a most liberal one it was. In addition to a full pardon, it offered to any informant freedom and a hundred *sestertia,* if he was a slave; if a free man, two hundred *sestertia.* But liberal as it was, it brought no response, and I have always felt that Cicero did not actually look for any; that it was intended merely to safeguard Pugnax and me.

So a number of uneventful days went by. We heard that the armies of Metellus Celer, in the valley of the Po, and of Antonius the consul, in Etruria, were being augmented by fresh levies and were pre-

paring for battle; and word came to us also that
Catilina, after stopping for a short time with Gaius
Flaminius Flamma, near Arretium, had joined
Manlius and had assumed the *fasces* and the *toga
praetexta,* announcing himself dictator. A number
of persons, hitherto unconnected with the plot, set
out to join him, among them one Aulus Fulvius, the
son of a senator. This young man, being arrested
while on his way to Etruria, was put to death by
order of his father, who declared that he had be-
gotten his son, not for Catilina against Rome, but
for Rome against Catilina. This act, which though
harsh was yet within the law, will serve to indicate
the depth of feeling that existed throughout the
City.

And it was while Rome was in this condition of
unrest, of tension, of anxiety, with nothing heard on
any hand save inquiries as to the progress of the
conspiracy, with groups of people in worried discussion on every corner, that the unbridled honesty
of Marcus Cato must needs choose this time to embarrass the man who was bending all his efforts to
save the State.

It came about thus. At the elections of the previous July, Decimus Silanus and Lucius Murena
were chosen consuls, to succeed Cicero and Antonius.
Laws had recently been passed increasing the pen-
alties for bribery at elections, and Cato, the invet-

erate enemy of political corruption—of which, the Gods know, there was plenty in Rome—heard rumors that Murena had spent gold freely for votes. Consequently, nothing would satisfy this most upright man but to bring charges against the consul-elect, and to take the case into the courts. Cicero, Caesar, and other leaders protested against the folly of throwing the City into a contested election at such a time, but Cato was inflexible; no appeal was of any avail—he would do it, and nothing could turn him aside. Cicero undertook to defend Murena and I have never been able sufficiently to admire the method he chose, for instead of being heavily serious, as most men would have been, he assumed a jocular tone, brought to bear all the resources of his wit and humor, and set the judges and the people laughing to such an extent that he not only secured Murena's acquittal, but even lightened in no small degree the feeling of strain which was over the City. Cato, to be sure, was unable to appreciate the wisdom of Cicero's course, and was heard to remark, with sour irony, "What a merry man we have for consul!" There is no denying that Cato, while invincibly honest, was not bright. But it was a remarkable performance of Cicero's, when one considers the unremitting anxiety that went to bed and rose again with him; and Gaius Caesar, who had perhaps a keener appreciation of strength and fortitude of mind than any other man in Rome, was outspoken in his congratulations.

Thus a fortnight passed, and one day a slave came to summon me to Cicero's home. Obeying the command, I found the consul in argument with Gaius Caesar, and it was the latter who addressed me.

"Tiberius," he said, "we who have the interests of Rome at heart feel that the consul should have always at his elbow a trusty bodyguard. He has told me of your birth, of your family, and we all know your alertness and your prowess with weapons, so I have sent for you to ask if you will undertake to watch over his safety."

Nothing could have pleased me more, and I said so.

"Very well," Caesar commended me. "You will continue to appear a slave, but since you are actually of patrician birth I add no threats in case of failure; I only appeal to your pride of family."

"With my life, *Domine*—Caesar, I mean." Confound that trick of speech! I could not rid myself of it. "If he dies, I die with him."

"That is not enough," said Caesar, instantly. "The meanest slave could do as much. It is not sufficient to purpose well; you must do well. He must not die! Understood?"

"Understood," I acknowledged, and Caesar concluded:

"It is well."

Thus it happened that I transferred my home from Catilina's to Cicero's and got to know the consul and his family intimately, nor can I ever say too much in favor of that great man. Oppressed with care though he was, he laid it all aside when he came home, and was ever jocular and pleasant within doors. Never were slaves better treated than his, and here I may say that though I knew him well until his death twenty years later, in all that time I never knew him to strike or scold a slave; in truth, his people dreaded the look of sorrow on their master's face more than they did the whip of the *lorarius,* and in the home on the Palatine that functionary held a sinecure. It has been said that Cicero was vain. This may be true, but at all events it was an innocent vanity; not pride, but rather a somewhat naïve and childlike pleasure in the consciousness of a task well done; nor was he ever jealous of others, but always ready to praise good work. I think that in the main what has been taken for vanity was merely a just appreciation of his own worth, combined with an utter freedom from that mock-modesty which makes us depreciate our own accomplishments. In one respect, however, Cicero's judgment was at fault; he always rated

Hortensius a finer orator than himself, but this was
not the verdict either of the people or of the best
judges. Altogether, the consul had a most charming personality, and was a man worthy of the utmost respect. Of the consul's wife I cannot speak
so highly; Terentia was harsh, overbearing, and of
a domineering nature. Further, she was of patrician
birth, and seemed to think she had married beneath
her in espousing a mere equestrian—as though any
descent were equal to inherent worth! Marcus,
their son, was a bright baby of some two years,
who was afterward a sore trial to his father, growing up to be a drunken, licentious gambler; it is only
fair to say, however, that after the father's death
young Marcus abandoned his evil ways and became
a worthy citizen. Quintus Cicero and his wife
Pomponia were frequent visitors, and I discovered
the former to be oddly contradictory in character.
He was a fop, a dandy, ever immaculate in his
person, oiled, bejeweled and scented to the last
degree, and wearing a short pointed beard in the
extreme of fashion, but for all that he gave indi-
cations of the force he later showed when a lieu-
tenant of Caesar's; Quintus Cicero's defence of his
camp against the Eburones and the Nervii deserves
a place among the great sieges of history. Of
Pomponia I can only say that she must have been
born of a Fury in an unlucky hour. She was quer-

ulous, fault-finding, sullen, and given to having her feelings hurt when no harm was intended; and when hurt she would either sulk or put on the air of a martyr. She had a thorough gift for making her associates uncomfortable, and had she been my wife I would have taken a stick to her back. Quintus, however, showed unfailing patience in dealing with her.

I have kept the best for the last—Tullia. Though but five years old, she had, when she chose, the gravity and seriousness of a full-grown woman. Thoughtful and studious, this child seemed to carry at the back of her eyes the wisdom of all the ages, yet like the consul she could be merry and playful, so that her joyous laugh rang through the *atrium*, and her father well called her the light of his home. When I was presented to her as her father's body-guard she looked at me gravely, then asked:

"You will not let any harm come to him?"

"No, little maid," I answered, with respect.

"You will always protect him?"

"With my life."

Still gazing intently into my eyes, she laid her hand in mine, gave me a serious smile, and replied:

"It is well. I like you; you are a good man."

After that there was no question; I was her devoted slave, and I am not ashamed to say that when, fifteen years later, word came of her untimely death,

I shut myself up and was unable to eat or to see anyone for three days.

But this is a tale of Rome's peril, not of Cicero's family life, and I must get back to my story.

One evening shortly before the Kalends of December *—I do not recall the exact date—Quintus Fabius Sanga came hotfoot to Cicero's home, demanding audience of the consul. Since I was at Cicero's elbow during all his waking hours, and slept across his door at night, necessarily I heard what Sanga had to tell. He was in such agitation that he could hardly keep still, but finally, being prevailed on to be seated, he began.

"It is known to you, my Tullius," he said, "that certain envoys of the Allobroges have come from Gallia Transalpina to Rome to seek relief from tribal debts owing to Flaccus and other bankers of the City." Cicero bowed agreement. "Early this morning," Sanga went on, "Tasgetius, chief of these envoys, came to me for advice, I being the Roman patron of their tribe. It seems that they were approached by one Publius Umbrenus, a freedman, who offered to show them how they might secure the desired relief. When Tasgetius expressed a natural interest, Umbrenus led the envoys to the home of Decimus Brutus—"

"Decimus Brutus!" exclaimed the consul, in as-

*December 1.

tonishment. *"Edepol!* I have always thought him an upright man."

"I believe he is," rejoined Sanga. "But his wife—?"

"Sempronia? Ah, yes! Proceed."

"Decimus being out of the City, the envoys met Sempronia, together with Publius Gabinius Capito. There was a conference, the gist of it being that Capito and Sempronia promised the Allobroges relief if they would play the part of men. The conspiracy was laid bare, and the Allobroges were assured that their debt would be not merely abated but entirely annulled if they would furnish certain troops of horse to aid Catilina and Manlius. The envoys, being unfamiliar with Roman politics, did not know what to say, so promised to take the matter under consideration, and came at once to me, their patron, for advice. And there you have the story."

When Sanga had finished, Cicero gazed for some time at the floor, then rose and paced the *atrium*, head bent, hands clasped behind him. At length he came to a halt before Sanga.

"My Quintus," he said, "you have done well. I believe the Gods are with Rome, and I myself will offer sacrifices to-morrow to Jupiter Stator and to Vesta.

"Meanwhile, do you find Tasgetius, explain to

him and to his companions the true state of affairs, and bid them pretend to fall in with Capito's proposal. Bid them obtain from him, and from any others who may be concerned in the plot, letters setting forth what the Allobroges are to do for Catilina, and what reward is promised; these letters should take the form of credentials to the tribe. Then bid them set out with all speed for their home, not failing to let me know beforehand the day and hour of their departure. And you may promise them relief from their debts, on the word of the consul. Farewell."

He extended his hand, pressed Sanga's, and courteously led the visitor to the door. Returning, he smiled at me, and I smiled also, for I thought I could read what was in his mind.

Some two or three days later, Gaius Caesar and Quintus Cicero came to the consul's late in the afternoon, and when they had conferred with Cicero the consul turned to me.

"Tiberius," he said, "you will arm yourself completely and report this evening to the praetor Lucius Flaccus at the Porta Flaminia; be there at the twelfth hour. He goes on an expedition, by my orders, and I want some trusty witness to report what occurs. Not that I doubt his truth, but it may be well to have confirmation. Place yourself under his command, and obey him in all things."

The Affair at the Mulvian Bridge

I bowed, and Caesar spoke to reassure me.

"We will guard the consul during your absence," he said, and I withdrew.

According to instructions, I went to the Porta Flaminia, where I found Flaccus and another praetor, Gaius Pomptinus, with some thirty soldiers, and shortly after dark we set out from the City, following the Via Flaminia. In the course of half an hour of marching we came to the Pons Mulvius, which crosses Tiber two or three miles above Rome, and here Flaccus halted us.

"Pomptinus," he commanded, "you will take half the men and cross the bridge, concealing yourselves on the other side. I will remain here, and when you hear me shout, then you will spread across the roadway and stop any who may come. I will close in behind them, so they will be taken between us."

Pomptinus and his men departed, and we heard the diminishing tramp of their footsteps die away across the bridge. Flaccus then ordered his men to hide themselves in the brush along the river-bank, and taking me with him bade me lie down in the long grass beside the road, close to the entrance of the bridge. He lay down by me, picking a spot a little back from the pavement and a few feet above it, so that we could look down and readily watch those who went by, ourselves being well concealed.

When we were settled:

"This is an idea of Cicero's," Flaccus told me. "Some of Catilina's friends have endeavored to suborn certain Gauls who are now in Rome, and the consul has received word that these Gauls will leave the City to-night, heading north. We are to arrest them and take them before him. Do you by chance know any of them?"

"No," I answered. "I have never seen them, to my knowledge."

"Well, no matter; we should be able to recognize them by their outlandish clothes. And it is probable that some of the conspirators will be with them. I see you have brought your cloak; that is well. Wrap yourself close against the evening chill; this is like to be a long wait. I am going to sleep; wake me when Ursa Parrhasis * says it is midnight, and I will take the second watch." He pulled his cloak over his head, turned on his side, drew up his knees, and in a few minutes his regular breathing told me that he slept.

It was an unpleasant night; not cold, but with a raw, damp chill in the air that struck through my woollen garments and from time to time caused me to shiver. The sky and the upper air were clear, but a low mist rose from Tiber, sending its coiling wreaths about us, leaving drops of moisture on our garments, our weapons, and the grass, and bringing

---

* The Great Dipper.

with it an uneasy hint of miasma. I drew my cloak over my mouth and nostrils to shut out the night air, and by this means gained some additional warmth; I did not dare, however, to wrap my whole head as Flaccus had done, for I must keep watch. Above me the stars shone clear and bright, and in the intervals of traffic I amused myself by picking out the various constellations, by noting their movement as I sighted them against a row of poplars that stood some distance off, and by wondering what these stars might really be. Some people claim that they are the windows through which the Gods look down upon us mortals from high Olympus, but that did not seem to me likely; if so, why should they move? I recalled an astrologer from Egypt who spent some time in our village when I was a youth; he explained that the sky was not really a dome above us, but was deep space, and that the stars were worlds like our own. But he did not tell us how they were kept in their places, and he said, also, that our world is not flat, but a ball, hanging in space, and that the sun and the stars appear to move because this ball turns daily on its axis, all of which is manifestly absurd, wherefore I could not believe his account of the stars. Well, it was not for me to settle the matter, and I turned my attention to the road.

The mist lay about knee-high to a man along this

part of the Via Flaminia, and strange it was to see the men and beasts and carts swimming above it, for there was considerable traffic into the City, though little away from it. Farmers from the country were bringing in grain and vegetables, cattle and sheep and hogs, to the markets, and torches flickered and flared for miles as the stream of food-stuffs took its way into the mighty City. The night was loud with the rumble of wheels, the shouts and talk of the men, and the lowing, bleating, and grunting of the animals, and once I heard a woman shrewishly berating her husband as they passed.

"Had you taken my advice," she snapped "this would never have occurred. We would still have the money. I told you from the very first. . . ." Her voice died away in the distance, and I grinned, thinking of Terentia; patrician or plebeian, there is a strong likeness in women.

Traveling outward, there were but few. Occasionally a litter passed, taking some noble for a few days at his country-seat, the bearers swinging along in perfect time, with the smooth, gliding gait which is so carefully taught them, and the relief padding close behind. From one such litter came a harsh voice cursing the slaves because the relief had been clumsy, so that the rider could feel them change places with the bearers; the voice promised a good dose of essence of elm, and vowed that if the offence were repeated the culprits would go to the farm or be sold into the quarries. A number of convivial parties went by, in various stages of drunkenness, and one such crowd fell into a quarrel and from that went into a free-for-all fight. This blocked traffic for a time, until the impatient farmers descended on the fighters with cudgels and basted all impartially. Once a drunken man came by alone, singing a ribald song at the top of his lungs; he missed the bridge entirely, lurched down the bank, and the song ended in a mighty splash. Presently he crawled up again, drenched but sober, and marched back the way he had come.

There was plenty of interest along the Via Flaminia, but at length traffic grew more sparse, until by midnight there was only an occasional cart, and when the time came I woke Flaccus, drew the hood of my cloak over my head, and went to sleep.

I was roused by a poke in the ribs, and as I sat up and rubbed my eyes the praetor said:

"I think they are coming."

Looking about, I saw in the east the first indication of dawn; it was not really that there was any light, but the stars were growing pale. A few birds chirped their morning song, and a frog boomed somewhere down the river. Off toward the City a group of torches flickered and bobbed against the dark background, and Flaccus and I lay close to the earth as they drew nearer. At length they were opposite where we hid, and only a few paces away, and I saw a dozen or so men in Gallic costume, and with them Titus Volturcius. I nudged Flaccus, and he responded with a faintly breathed:

"I see."

When the party was about at the middle of the bridge Flaccus leaped up with a ringing shout, there came a scrambling rush of feet below us, and our men, spreading across the bridge, charged at a trot along it. Pomptinus was alert, and the travelers, caught between two forces, immediately surrendered; the Gauls had been warned what to expect. That is, all yielded but Volturcius; taken by surprise, he thought us a band of robbers, and drawing his sword he laid about him viciously. He wounded one of our men, but another knocked the weapon from his hand, whereupon, recognizing us for soldiers, he rushed to the parapet and tried to fling himself into the river. Seized and brought back, he struggled and swore, but was overpowered and his arms were tied behind him, when he submitted without further trouble. All of a sudden the courage went out of him, and he dropped on his knees, piteously and in abject terror begging the praetors to save his life. He implored them to let him go, to have mercy upon him, not to take him before the consul; and he promised them all his money if they would but spare him. I was ashamed that a Roman could be so craven—what is death, compared to dishonor?—and I turned my eyes from the sight.

"It is for the consul to decide your fate," Flaccus told him. "Forward, march!" And we set out for Rome, the soldiers half carrying, half dragging the wretched conspirator.

It was broad daylight, though the sun had not fully risen, when we reached Cicero's home, and on demand of Flaccus were admitted, our party pretty well filling the *atrium,* where Caesar and the consul's brother sat before the door of one of the sleeping-rooms. Being summoned, Cicero came from this room, taking a chair and commanding that the prisoners be ranged before him. I noticed Tullia, flushed and tousled from her dreams, peering at us from behind the curtain of her bed-room, and catching her eye, I nodded and smiled at her, whereat she smiled in return, blowing me a kiss from her rosy little fingers. *Mehercle,* what a beautiful child she was!

Now Tasgetius, chief of the envoys, was speaking.

"Oh, Consul," he began, "we have obeyed your commands. We pretended sympathy with the plot, and were introduced to this man—" indicating Volturcius "—and to a number of others—"

"Can you name them?" Cicero interrupted.

"I cannot name all who are in the conspiracy," replied Tasgetius. "Those we met, those who gave us letters, were Lentulus Sura, Gaius Cethegus, Publius Statilius, Gabinius Capito, and Quintus Coeparius."

The consul threw a look of distress toward Gaius Caesar.

"Per Deos Immortales!" he said. "The noblest families of Rome! And Lentulus is one of our praetors." Caesar nodded gravely in response.

After a moment's thought, the consul went on:

"Pomptinus, do you take ten men, find those whose names you have just heard, and bring them before me."

Saluting, Pomptinus called his men and departed, and Cicero turned to Flaccus.

"Did you secure the letters?" he asked.

"They are here." And Flaccus handed over a box which he had received from Tasgetius.

Opening the box, Cicero took therefrom a number of tablets, bound with cord and sealed, and his brother and Caesar moved closer to look.

"That is Lentulus Sura's seal," the latter pointed out. "Do you not recognize the portrait of his grandfather?"

Cicero nodded.

"A most upright man," he answered, sadly. "One would think that the sight of that likeness would have recalled Lentulus from his treason. How the spirit of that old man must grieve to see his grandson a partaker of such villainy! Here is Cethegus' seal, too."

"And those of Coeparius, and Statilius, and Capito," said Quintus Cicero. He drew his dagger and extended the hilt to the consul, who looked inquiringly at it. "Are you not going to cut the cords and read what is written on the wax?" asked Quintus.

The consul shook his head.

"Not now," he answered. "I will open the tablets before the Senate; not sooner, lest someone claim that I have substituted others for the genuine." Replacing the letters in the box, he drew out a parchment roll, opened it, and scanned it. "The oath of the conspirators," he said. "Written and signed in blood. Oh, Vesta, Preserver of the Hearth, these names!" He dropped the roll and buried his face in his hands, and when he looked up I saw that his cheeks were wet with tears. "Oh, Jupiter, Father of All," he prayed aloud, "grant me strength to do what must be done!"

Caesar laid an arm about the consul's shoulders, whispering in his ear, and Cicero, regaining his composure, nodded.

"Flaccus," he said, "send messengers to call a meeting of the Senate for this morning. Bid them be in the Temple of Concord by the fourth hour."

Bowing, the praetor went on his errand, and with that Volturcius, who had been trembling and shaking in the rear of the crowd, pressed forward and rushed toward the consul. Instantly Caesar, Quintus Cicero, and I, our daggers drawn, blocked his path, but he dropped on his knees and we stepped back, for his hands were still tied behind him.

"Oh, Consul," he begged, his voice quavering, "have mercy! I was drawn into the plot—I do not seek Rome's downfall, I do not, I do not! I was misled, beguiled, cheated—Catilina lied to me, he lied, he lied. I am not guilty, I swear by all the Gods I am not! I . . . I will tell all . . . I swear I will. Have mercy, have pity! Spare my life; have me beaten with rods, exiled, sold into slavery —anything!—but let me live. I will reveal the whole plot, I will hold back nothing, if you will but spare my life. I swear it by the Immortal Gods, by the sacred name of Jupiter Stator! Have mercy!"

Quintus Cicero turned away, a look of disgust on his countenance.

"Pah!" he said. "And this was born in Rome, of Roman parents!"

I saw the consul's face twitch as if in pain, and an expression of contempt spread over the features of the Gauls; alone of all the company, Gaius Caesar looked on unmoved. Getting no response to his agonized pleadings, Volturcius let his voice trail off into silence, and at length Cicero answered, gravely:

"It is not for me to judge you, Titus. You will go before the Senate, like the others, and they will decide your fate." He gave a signal, and two soldiers lifted the craven and led him, still trembling and sobbing, to a distant part of the room.

"It makes one feel sick and unhappy," remarked the consul, in a sad voice, "to see a fellow-creature thus prize life above honor. I like to think that were I given such a choice I would behave better."

"You would, my Tullius," replied Caesar. "It is not in you to be craven." And indeed he spoke the truth; Gaius Caesar had a keener insight than the fools who called Marcus Cicero a coward. No coward would have faced this conspiracy as he did; no coward would have defied Marcus Antonius as he did years later; nor did ever the most courageous meet inevitable death more calmly than that same Cicero.

There was some further discussion, and presently the slaves served breakfast, handing around the usual bread and cheese and wine, and after all had eaten, Cicero, Caesar and Quintus Cicero retired to the consul's office for more debate. Volturcius was sent for, to be questioned, and they all appeared again about the third hour, when Pomptinus and his men returned, bringing Lentulus Sura, Cethegus, Statilius, and Capito.

"Coeparius somehow got wind of what was on foot," Pomptinus reported, "and has fled for Apulia. I dispatched four men on swift horses, and they should overtake him before long; he went by litter, and had not been gone an hour when we reached his house."

"We will wait until it is time to set out for the Temple of Concord," the consul decided. "Then if he has not arrived we will proceed without him."

He questioned those whom the praetor had brought, and they one and all declared themselves innocent, protesting that their accusers lied, that the whole story was a fabrication. Knowing what I did, I was surprised that the consul failed to mention the box of letters, but he doubtless had his own reasons, and in the course of half an hour or so there came a knock at the street door and Coeparius was ushered in, guarded by three soldiers and a centurion. He changed countenance and grew pale at sight of the company, but was not given a chance to speak. Rising from his chair, Cicero announced:

"It is time to go. Tiberius, you will keep close by me, even in the Senate chamber. Flaccus and Pomptinus, bring these men, and guard them closely against any possible rescue. Come, Lentulus." He held out his hand to Lentulus Sura—this mark of honor was due to one who was both praetor and ex-consul—and so we started, Cicero leading Lentulus in friendly manner, though at the same time grave and quiet, and the rest following in a compact body. Outside the door Cicero halted for a moment to speak with one Gaius Sulpicius, a praetor, who nodded and hurried off, then on we went once more.

Down the slope of the Palatine we marched, grim-faced and silent, troubled in our minds, and so along the Vicus Tuscus, and past the foot of the Capitoline. Then along the Vicus Jugarius, past the Temple of Saturn, and past the Old Shops into the Forum. An excited crowd had been collecting at our heels, talking and chattering, and as we continued our solemn march across the end of the Forum, people came running from all directions, and the crowd grew like a gathering snowball, not to leave us until, with grave and measured tread, we mounted the steps of the Temple of Concord and entered the Senate chamber.

CHAPTER IX

Of the Trial of the Five; and of the Tullianum

NOTHING could be imagined more impressive than the scene in the Temple of Concord, that fateful morning of December. The great nave of the Temple, floored and walled with the richest woods, and adorned with statues by the most famous sculptors; the long rows of benches on which sat Rome's greatest men, to the number of six hundred or more; the high altar, before which the consul had his place; the armed guards surrounding the accused, who by their uneasy bearing showed their sense of the peril in which they stood; all these combined to form a picture that will live in the memories of those who were there to see—and who themselves lived to remember it.

But now Cicero was on his feet, and in a brief speech he outlined the events of which I have told; the attempt to suborn the Allobroges, their pretended acceptance of the conspiracy, and the capture of the party on the Pons Mulvius. Flaccus, Pomptinus and I were called to give evidence in support of his words, and Tasgetius, being questioned, repeated his statement.

"Lentulus Sura told us," he added, "that the Sibylline Books and a number of soothsayers had prophesied that a third member of the Cornelian gens should hold kingdom and sovereignty over Rome; that two portents, ten years apart, should occur, and that ten years after the second of these portents should come the rule of a Cornelian. Twenty years ago, he assured us, was the first of these omens, the burning of the Capitol; ten years after that came the trial and acquittal of the Vestals; and now a decade had passed since that trial. Cinna and Sulla had held the rule, and he, Publius Cornelius Lentulus Sura, was the third of his family to contend for the sovereignty. Therefore, he said, naught could be more clear than that he was favored of the Gods, and would win the reward he sought."

A murmur of anger ran through the benches when Tasgetius ended, but it was cut short as Gaius Sulpicius entered the Temple followed by a crowd of soldiers, each loaded down with weapons. The senators looked on amazed while with recurrent clash of steel these arms were thrown down, to make a vast heap in one corner of the room, and when Sulpicius and his men had retired, the consul got to his feet once more.

"I sent the praetor to search the home of Cethegus," he said. "Oh, Conscript Fathers, you can see for yourselves what fruit he has plucked from that tree. Gaius Cethegus, stand forth!"

Burly, red-faced, and arrogant, Cethegus swaggered forward a few steps.

"Cethegus," pursued the consul, "you are accused of being a party to this conspiracy. What have you to say?"

"Much!" boomed Cethegus, insolently. "First, I am a patrician of Rome, of senatorial rank; by what right does an equestrian, a new man, an upstart, accuse me? Who are you to sit in judgment on your betters? Can your house show waxen masks of curule ancestors? No! As for these arms, when was it ever a crime for a Roman citizen to own sword and dagger? May not a free-born Roman arm his slaves if he sees fit?"

"Not against the State," retorted Cicero. "And when he arms the slaves of others he lays himself open to grave suspicion. And we can all see that here are ten times enough weapons to arm your entire family."

"As for that," Cethegus answered, "I have always loved good cutlery, and have collected it for its own sake—for the pleasure I find in handling good craftsmanship. If that is your best evidence of my guilt—of my alleged guilt—bid your myrmidons stand fast and let me go."

Turning to Flaccus, Cicero held out his hand, in

which the praetor placed the box of letters. Taking therefrom a tablet, the consul asked Cethegus:

"Is that your seal?"

Cethegus paled, hesitated for an instant, then said:

"Even so."

"Bear witness, oh, Conscript Fathers," said the consul, "that he acknowledges the seal, and that the cord is unbroken." Taking my dagger, he cut the cord, opened the tablets, and read: " 'To the Senate and People of the Allobrogian nation, greeting. Your envoys will tell you what has been promised to them and to you. These present words will confirm that promise, and I beg that you will carry out what your envoys have promised in your name. The Gods be with you. Farewell. Gaius Cassius Cethegus.' " He ceased, closed the tablets, and bent a stern look on Cethegus, while a rumbling growl ran along the benches.

For a moment Cethegus tried to outstare the consul, tried to speak in answer. But no words came; he dropped his eyes to the floor and stood silent, all his arrogance forsaking him.

The consul then took from the box another letter, and Statilius acknowledged the seal; when read, it proved of much the same tenor as Cethegus', and Statilius admitted that it was his own. A third was then produced, and Cicero asked Lentulus Sura:

"Do you recognize that seal?"

Lentulus nodded, unable to speak.

"The portrait of your grandfather, is it not?"

Lentulus nodded again.

"A most illustrious man," said the consul, "and one who greatly loved his country and his fellow-citizens. Even though silent, his image should have restrained you from such wickedness." Being read, the letter was of the same purport as the others, and Cicero asked: "Have you aught to say?"

"Much," replied Lentulus, and rose. "I have much to say." He paused a moment, seeming to arrange his thoughts, then, impressive and somewhat threatening of manner: "Tasgetius, can you in honor claim that I have myself made such proposals to you? Dare you assert that my seal was not forged? Can you declare with certainty, in the sight of the Immortal Gods, that you know me to be guilty? Dare you say that I have tried to betray my country? Do you not admit that you may be mistaken? Before Jupiter the All-Father, answer!"

Steadily and without hesitation, Tasgetius made reply:

"In the sight of Jupiter and the Gods of my own people, I do so dare, I do so assert."

Lentulus seemed taken aback, but he turned to Volturcius.

"Titus Volturcius," he said, "dare you assert that

I am a traitor to Rome and to my people? Think well; remember that this is no common cause; that we stand in the presence of Jupiter the All-Seeing, and that your answer will be written against you in the Book of the Fates. Think well of all that you have seen and done before you answer; think well what treason and betrayal mean; then speak."

Volturcius cringed and whimpered, and Cicero rose.

"Conscript Fathers," he said, "I think that Volturcius holds back lest he convict himself by his reply. Have I your permission to grant him a pardon if he reveals all that he knows?"

A chorus of assent replied, and Cicero turned to the craven.

"Titus Volturcius," he said, "you have heard, and you are safe—your life is safe from Rome's vengeance. Speak, then, and in the name of the Immortals, tell the truth, whether it be for or against your associates."

Instead of answering directly, Volturcius drew from his tunic a letter and displayed it to Lentulus.

"Is that your seal?" he asked.

"Forged," replied Lentulus, scornfully.

Cutting the cord, Volturcius read:

" 'To Catilina at Faesulae. S. V. B. E. E. V. Who I am, you will learn from him whom I have sent to you. Take care to behave like a man, con-

sider how far you have gone, and provide what is
necessary. Take care to gather to yourself the aid
of everyone, even the weakest. *Vale.'* "

All eyes were turned toward Lentulus, who
seemed collecting his forces to speak in his own
defence. And even then he might have prevailed,
for he was no mean orator, and as patrician, ex-
consul, and praetor, his words would have borne
weight; the Senate were reluctant to credit such
things of one of their own number. But suddenly
the power of the Gods was manifest, for though
he thrice opened h s mouth to speak, no words came
forth; pale, his fat cheeks quivering, he gasped for
air, then to the amazement of all his conscience
overwhelmed him and he dropped his face in his
hands, groaning aloud:

"I am guilty; do with me what you will."

Next Gabinius Capito was questioned, and though
at first he answered impudently, denying everything,
at length he too broke down, admitting his guilt.
Coe-parius needed no cross-examination; of weaker
fibre than the others, he admitted everything when
first summoned, and the case was complete. But
indeed the very manner and bearing of the accused
would have convicted them; pale, silent, with downcast eyes they sat, and any true man could read guilt
in their ashen cheeks and quivering lips, in their
stealthy sidelong glances at their companions, so

that in truth they seemed not so much betrayed as betraying one another.

For the sake, though, of irrefutable proof, of conviction beyond all doubt, the conspirators and the Gauls were removed to another part of the building, and Volturcius was questioned. He controlled himself enough to answer plainly, and told straightforwardly the whole tale of the conspiracy, giving the names of all concerned.

"And there," he closed, whirling on me with extended arm and pointing finger, "there stands one of the most guilty of all. Catilina's slave and bodyguard, he was privy to our councils, he kept watch during our meetings, he carried arms to Cethegus, he was of constant aid to the plot. Let him not go unpunished!"

For a moment I felt my knees shake, but instantly Cicero was afoot, speaking.

"It is true," he said, "that Tiberius the gladiator was of the conspiracy, but he experienced a change of heart, and it is due to him that I am here to-day. He it was who gave warning of the plan of Vargunteius and Cornelius to assassinate me, thereby enabling me to frustrate them. And since then he has done me good service. Tiberius has deserved well of the State, and should be rewarded, not punished. In any case, he can claim immunity under your decree of some time since."

Caesar rose in his place.

"I can confirm what the consul has said of Tiberius' services," he remarked briefly, and sat down.

"So also can I," said Quintus Cicero, and Flaccus added:

"And I."

"I would like to ask," spoke up Sanga, "if Tiberius agrees with what Volturcius has told us of the plot."

"Up to the time of Catilina's flight from the City," I answered, "yes. Since then, I have little or no knowledge of their doings."

Cato got to his feet.

"I object," he said, "to taking the evidence of a slave against Roman patricians. Even admitting that they are guilty, as I firmly believe, we should not ask a slave to testify against them."

"It does no harm to inquire," Sanga remarked, to which Cato retorted:

"It sets a bad precedent."

"That question may be dismissed, I think," Cicero offered. "It remains for us to decide what steps shall be taken with regard to the five and to the others whom Volturcius has accused. We are agreed, I think, that their guilt is established, and it rests with us to determine their punishment."

But Gaius Caesar was on his feet.

"Oh, Conscript Fathers," he said, "may I claim

your attention? Before we proceed with this other
business, there is one matter I would call to your
notice, lest it be overlooked. We have among us a
man who by his native genius has raised himself
from equestrian to senatorial rank; who, though
born without the City, yields to none in his love
for Rome, in his loyalty to the State; who by sheer
force of intellect and devotion has lifted himself
to the highest office within that State. This man
has borne the abuse and hatred of the nobles, and
for months has gone in daily, nay, hourly, danger of
assassination. But for neither abuse nor peril has
he flinched one step from the path of devotion, and
by his wisdom and his steadfastness he has pre-
served our lives from the dagger-men of Catilina,
our homes from the destruction of fire, and our
wives and children from rape and slaughter. Shall
we not pay honor to such a man? Is it not fitting
that our highest praise be given him? Never in all
Rome's history has any man done such great service
to the State, and therefore I propose for him an
honor such as never yet has been paid to any civilian,
to any save some victorious general. I propose a
day of solemn thanksgiving to the Immortal Gods
in the name of Marcus Tullius Cicero, because under
Them he has delivered the City from conflagration,
the citizens from massacre, and Italia from civil
war. Conscript Fathers, is it your will?"

And I saw the consul's face flush with pleasure as
one and all the senators leaped to their feet and with
right hands extended toward him they thundered:

"So be it! Thus is it decreed!"

The rest of that long day was given to business,
to a debate regarding the course to be pursued.
No recess for luncheon was taken, nor—even more
remarkable—was the siesta hour observed. Slaves
brought food, the senators taking it in their hands
and eating while the debate went on, and again and
again the hourglass was turned. The other conspirators, it was agreed, should be placed under
arrest, and soldiers were sent to take them, but came
back with the word that, alarmed, these men had
fled the City. The Senate, therefore, must be content with passing an edict of outlawry against them,
and this was done. The question came up of the
punishment to be meted out to the ones in captivity,
but this was too momentous for a hurried decision,
and it was agreed to hold them prisoner and to
meet again, two days later, to decide their fate.
Accordingly, Lentulus Sura was given in charge of
Publius Lentulus Spinther, the aedile; Cethegus went
with Quintus Cornificius; Gaius Caesar took Statilius; Gabinius Capito went with Marcus Crassus;
and Gnaeus Terentius took the guardianship of
Coeparius. And the sun having set, the meeting
broke up.

The Trial of the Five

Many of the senators crowded around the consul, praising and congratulating him, pressing in to shake his hand, nor was it difficult to see that he was pleased. I do not mean that he swelled with pride like a turkey-cock, but who would not be gratified by praise from men who had hitherto showered down abuse, contempt, and hatred? Cicero won their hearts as long before he had won their minds—small blame to him if he was pleased!

At length the crowd filtered away, all but the few who would accompany the consul home: Gaius Caesar, Quintus Cicero, Flaccus, Pomptinus, Cato, and half a dozen others. Cicero turned to me.

"Well, Tiberius," he said, "this has been a great day. A solemn thanksgiving to the Gods! That will be something to relate to Tullia, eh, my Redhead?"

I smiled at the thought.

"I can see her eyes dance and shine when she hears it," I answered, and he clapped me on the back in friendly fashion. I saw Cato and some of the others lift their eyebrows at such familiarity with a slave, but nothing was said; doubtless they put it down to a natural exuberance coming from pleasure and release from strain.

But as we left the Temple of Concord we saw that the Forum was jammed from side to side and from end to end with a crowd of people so close-packed that I could have walked on their heads, not setting foot to the ground. A great shout went up, demanding knowledge of the conspiracy, and a roar of "Cicero! Cicero!" rolled echoing back and forth from temple to temple and from wall to wall. Cicero halted on the steps.

"I must speak to them," he said. "And, oh Immortal Gods, how weary I am!"

"Bid them disperse," Cato suggested. "Promise to speak to them to-morrow. You have done enough for to-day."

I was surprised at this mark of human sympathy in Cato, and Cicero must have been, as well, but he only shook his head, saying:

"They have a right to know. Flaccus, have the soldiers clear a way to the Rostra and hold torches. I will speak."

His command was obeyed, and crossing the Forum, the consul mounted the Rostra, where he spoke for perhaps half an hour, delivering what is known as the Third Oration Against Catilina, in which he told all that I have related of the past forty-eight hours. As always, the people hung on his words, and when he had finished, a mighty roar beat upward to the dark sky, the crowd hailing him: "Savior! Deliverer! Father of Rome!"

And it was with difficulty that the soldiers could thrust a path through the crowd to get us home,

so dense was the throng that pressed around to see
the consul, to do him reverence, to touch his garments in awe and adoration.

We did not go that night to the home on the
Palatine, for it was occupied by the Vestals. Once
each year the priestesses of Vesta, with other patrician women, celebrate in the house of some magistrate the rites of the Bona Dea, and from this celebration all males are excluded with utmost rigor.
Therefore Cicero asked if Flaccus could entertain
him for the night, and the praetor acceded gladly;
he seemed to feel that he would be honored. So
it was to Flaccus' home that we went, and there
passed a busy evening, for not only did Cicero's
intimate friends accompany him thither, but scores
of others dropped in from time to time to offer their
congratulations and to express admiration of the
crafty manner in which the plotters had been trapped
and forced to convict themselves. Until midnight
there was no time when the *atrium* was not crowded,
when the buzz of talk did not fill its remotest corner,
and it seemed as though the enmity between patrician and equestrian had been laid aside, for senators
and knights mingled freely and gladly, outspoken
in their praise of what the consul had done.

"*Edepol*, Tullius," said Decimus Silanus, the consul-elect, "your son will not be called a new man
—not with a father who held the consulate and for

whom a thanksgiving was decreed. None of the most ancient houses can boast such an image as will be his to show. And when the time comes, we will make him consul, for your sake if not for his own."

The consul smiled with gratification at the hearty applause which greeted this sentiment, but immediately his face became grave once more.

"We must not forget, though, my friends," he reminded them, "that our task is but half done. Catilina still lives, and has two full legions at his command. The danger is by no means past."

"We will attend to him in due course," Marcus Cato said. "It will not be difficult, now that we Optimates are awakened to our peril." And with this the others agreed.

But at length the house emptied itself of visitors, or nearly so; two only remained, Quintus Catulus and Gaius Piso, who asked and received a private audience. As the consul's bodyguard, I was necessarily present at the interview, and it is putting it mildly to say that I was shocked when I learned what they wanted. Catulus hated Gaius Caesar, who had defeated him for the office of Pontifex, and Piso hated him because Caesar had attacked Piso when the latter was on trial for extortion; and now they appealed to Cicero to have Caesar also convicted of treason. The Allobrogian envoys could easily be persuaded, they said, to include Caesar's name with those of the conspirators, and they themselves would furnish whatever money might be necessary, up to a thousand *sestertia*. And Volturcius would require no more than a suggestion to make him swear that Caesar was of the conspiracy. This was not said straight out, of course, but with much hinting and circumlocution; the meaning was plain, however; Cicero was to bribe Volturcius and the envoys, and to keep for himself whatever might be left of that great sum. I felt my heart grow hot within me as I listened, but a glance at Cicero's face calmed me; grim and silent he sat, hearing them out, letting them convict themselves, and when they had finished he turned to me.

"Tiberius," he said, "show these gentlemen to the street." There was the faintest possible emphasis on the word "gentlemen," but that was all.

"But . . . but . . ." stammered Piso. "Tullius . . . we might make it two thousand . . . that would leave. . . ." He got no further; I had been given a task much to my liking, and with naked sword I advanced upon the two. Their exit was rapid, but scarcely dignified.

Back from closing the door, I found Cicero gazing sadly at the glowing coals within the brazier.

"Tiberius," he addressed me, "the baseness of men is beyond all credence. At times I despair of doing any good—I feel that my efforts are futile. Public treason, private treachery, lust for gain, falsehood, cruelty, the conscienceless traffic in votes—to what is the State coming? I seem to see Rome crashing in ruin before some younger, sturdier people, even as Carthage fell before Rome; perhaps some tribe of Gallia or Germania sowing salt above Her ruins. Wealthy, glorious, powerful, mistress of the world, She carries within Her the seeds of internal strife, of destruction, just as some man, blooming with health and strong of frame, may bear a deadly cancer gnawing at his vitals."

"There are some noble souls within the State," I offered.

"A few," he made acknowledgment. "But not many," was the mournful addition. "Tiberius," he went on, "I do not know whether Rome is to live or to die; in either case, it will not be in my time or yours. But this I can say; if the State is to endure, it is in the hands of one man to decide; one who was here to-night."

He bent his gaze on the coals as though striving to read there the answer to his doubts, while I ran over in my mind the visitors. But I could think of none who seemed to me great enough to warrant such a prophecy, until a sudden thought struck me.

"Yourself, Tullius!" I cried.

He smiled sadly, shaking his head.

"I thank you, Tiberius, but it is a greater than I. Gaius Caesar."

"Gaius Caesar!" I exclaimed, for though I was ready to admit that this man was a leader, I saw in him no such giant as Cicero found.

"No other," the consul assured me. "You may perhaps live to see it. But it is late; let us get to bed." Rising, he bade me summon Flaccus, who led the way to our sleeping-room, where Cicero retired to bed, while I stretched out across the door, thinking of his words, unable to credit that he was not mistaken. Years afterward, I was obliged to grant that his insight was keener than my own.

The atmosphere of the City on the following day was a strange one. The tension was somewhat relieved, to be sure, and the anxiety which had been so apparent during the last few weeks was no more to be seen. It was as though Rome felt the danger to be over—a feeling that was by no means justified, in view of the fact that Catilina was preparing to hurl twelve thousand armed men against the walls. However, it was perhaps not remarkable that the people felt secure, a portion of the conspirators being under arrest and the others in voluntary exile; not since Sulla's day had so many senators and knights fled from Rome in the space of twelve hours! But if the sense of fear had left us, its place was taken by one of curious, unnamed foreboding. And in truth there was cause for such a feeling; here were five men from the noblest families of Rome, under arrest and convicted of the basest treason against the State. What would —what could—be done with them? It was unthinkable that they should be set free; they would simply go to their leader and fight in his army, and even if exiled they would find means to join him. But there was no provision under the Roman law for holding them prisoner; we had no suitable prisons, and private custody can be used for only a limited time. And it was incredible that the consul should order their execution; even though the Senate had passed the Extreme Decree, still the Sempronian law forbids the execution of any citizen without appeal to the people. Would they so appeal? Would we have a public trial of the five? In the unsettled condition of the public mind, with no one knew how many slaves and gladiators ready for instant uprising, to permit such a trial would be most unwise. Or would Cicero take the law into his own hands, defy future enemies, future condemnation, and mete out the punishment of treason? The question was freely debated throughout the City, nor were there lacking many to point out to the consul where his duty lay; no great man ever yet lacked swarms of volunteer advisers, and there are always plenty who are wiser than the wisest. I had opportunity to see and hear what went on, for I was much abroad during the day, being sent hither and thither on errands for the consul, so that I spent no small number of hours traversing the streets.

During my goings to and fro I picked up snatches of conversation which led me to believe that Lentulus' friends were planning a rescue, and a few minutes after reaching this conclusion I had it confirmed, if not directly, at least by implication.

While crossing the Forum Velabrum, I chanced to meet Pugnax, and stopped to speak with him.

"Ha, Tiberius!" he hailed me. "What news?"

I told him what was uppermost in my mind, and he nodded.

"It seems probable," he acknowledged. "In fact, I was on my way to find you, with some such notion in my own head. You remember Hylas, that huge yellow-haired brute who is Cethegus' chief bodyguard? Like master, like man! Well, he came to our house an hour ago, held a long private interview with Fulvia, and when he had gone she sent for me and bade me hold myself in readiness for instant fighting. From all of which I conclude that a rescue is being instigated."

"Will you obey?"

"*Per Deos Immortales!*" he snorted. "Is it likely? With freedom and a hundred *sestertia* in sight? Did the Gods make my brain of clay? I was

on the road to see you, to ask you to present me
to Cicero, that he might give me a place with the
soldiers of the State."

"I am on an errand that I may not abandon," I
told him. "But you need no introduction; Cicero
has not forgotten you; he is his own *nomenclator*.
Go direct to him with your request; he is at Flaccus' home."

With a wave of the hand, we separated, and later
in the day I saw my friend with a body of soldiers
who were on guard in the Forum, when he told me
that Cicero had placed guards at the homes where
the conspirators were held, at the Temple of Concord, on the Palatine and Capitoline, and at other
strategic points about the City.

All that day, Flaccus' home was a very beehive
for activity, with friends and messengers coming
and going through the long hours, with a constant
buzz of argument and talk, and a general air of
bustle and anxiety. Late in the afternoon, however,
we had a visitor who, though unexpected, cheered us
greatly, and I think resolved any doubts the consul
may have had as to his duty.

About the ninth hour, when I was returning from
an errand, a litter drew up at the door just as I
reached there. Going over to it, I had the pleasure
of aiding Terentia to alight—if pleasure it could
be called, for I disliked her intensely. However, I

was always scrupulously courteous in my dealings with her, and now I offered my arm to help her dismount. Entering the house, she went directly to the *atrium,* where she pushed through the crowd about her husband and spoke to him in a loud, aggressive tone, quite regardless of the fact that Cato was talking with him at the time.

"Marcus," she said, "the Vestals have sent me to tell you of an omen that we observed last night. As you know, the rites of the Goddess demand that when the sacred meal and oil have been sacrificed, the sacred fire be allowed to go out, that it may be kindled anew for another year by friction of apple and maple woods.

"Last night—early this morning, rather—the sacrifices being made, we allowed the fire to die out, then when the ashes were cold we made the supplications of the ritual, and Septimia prepared the sacred fire-sticks. But ere ever she brought them together, lo! of its own accord the fire blazed up anew. Great was our astonishment and great the discussion, but in the end the priestesses decided that Vesta, Preserver of the Hearth, sent this omen as a sign that she approves of what you are doing to save the hearths of Her chosen City. And they bade me carry this message to you. Farewell." And she departed as unceremoniously as she had come.

It may well be understood that this sign of favor from the most holy of Rome's protectors meant no little rejoicing, and the consul was seen to bow his head in silent prayer. Doubtless he was thanking the Goddess for Her approval and encouragement, for though many of Rome's greatest men are secret if not open scoffers, he was always most devout. And indeed, even of the scoffers and agnostics, I have never known any to deny the power and the holiness of Vesta.

The morrow, the Nones of December,* opened bright and clear, but before the Senate met in the Temple of Concord the sky was overcast with rolling masses of dark gray clouds that hid the sun and spread a gloom over the whole City, and a chill wind struck down from the hills to set us shivering; it was as though the Gods, knowing what was to come, sent us a day fitting the day's events. By the third hour the senators were in their places, and Decimus Silanus made a brief address to state the purpose of the meeting. Cicero then rose, addressed Silanus—this courtesy was due the consul-elect—and asked his opinion as to what should be done with the convicted men. Silanus replied in a few words, voting for their death. One after another of the senators was called upon, each giving the same verdict until it came the turn of Gaius Caesar. He

* December 5.

spoke at some length, calling attention to the Sempronian law, and then advanced another proposition.

"I would not have you think, oh Conscript Fathers," he said, "that I am moved by any weak or womanish compassion for these most evil men. But should we violate this law, there will be many to condemn us, to say that we are arrogating to ourselves a power that is not justly in our hands. You will recall that it was thus the infamous Thirty began in Athens—by exceeding their lawful powers in order to punish wicked men. And from that they passed to the oppression of upright citizens, which many will fear of us if we do this thing.

"As for my argument arising from soft-heartedness, let me say that I am in favor of a punishment more severe than you have advocated. I would confiscate the goods of these men, and incarcerate the offenders for life in some slave-prison, making it unlawful for any to seek their release, at any future time whatever. Thus we shall be within the law, yet punish them more bitterly than by death, for what is death compared to poverty, disgrace, and a perpetual dungeon in company with earth's vilest slaves?" He spoke further in this same strain, and it was easy to see that he had vast influence over the minds of his hearers; indeed, so great was his eloquence, so great the power of his personality, that when he had finished Silanus rose and asked permission to change his former verdict, saying that he agreed with Caesar.

Then others spoke, till Cicero got to his feet and delivered his Fourth Oration Against Catilina, so well known to all lovers of great literature. Briefly, it was an impassioned speech, pointing out the wickedness of which the five were guilty, calling upon the Conscript Fathers to remember their duty to the City, and offering to take on his own shoulders any blame for violating the Sempronian law.

"In truth," he said, "I feel with Caesar, that these men, having conspired against the State, can no longer be regarded as citizens. But this most gentle and merciful man does not hesitate to condemn Lentulus to eternal darkness and imprisonment, and to establish a law forbidding any to alleviate his punishment. Yet if we are very rigorous, we shall be considered merciful, but if we choose to be kind, we shall endure the reputation of utmost cruelty."

Much more he said, and was followed by Cato, who spoke to the same effect though with less eloquence, and these two men swept the Senate before them to a verdict that was all but unanimous.

The meeting then broke up, Cicero gave some orders, and, accompanied only by myself and a few guards, the consul went to the home of Publius Spinther, where Lentulus was confined. We found the conspirator seated in the *atrium*, reading a comedy of Plautus, and as we entered he looked up and asked:

"Is it decided?"

Cicero bowed without speaking, and Lentulus must have read his face, for he inquired:

"Death?"

Again Cicero bowed, and Lentulus, rising, calmly rolled up the scroll and replaced it in the cabinet, saying only:

"It is just."

"One thing," said Cicero. "As a praetor of the City, you cannot be punished while you hold office—"

"I waive that," Lentulus interrupted. "I am guilty, and it is just that I be punished."

"Come, then."

Cicero extended his hand, which Lentulus took, and hand in hand they left the house, we others following at their heels.

Crowds had gathered in the streets and in the Forum, but for the most part they gave way before us, drawing back silently to let us pass. One man, indeed, stepped forward and barred our path, shaking his fist in Lentulus' face and bellowing:

"Traitor!"

I had never thought too well of Lentulus, but his calm and dignified bearing at this dire time had roused my admiration and my pity, so that I sprang forward and struck the insulter in the face with my clenched fist, putting my weight into the blow. The man rolled senseless and bleeding in the gutter, and I learned afterward that his jaw was broken and his cheek-bone crushed in. Would that I had slain him!

Reaching the Carcer of Ancus Martius, we found there the other conspirators, guarded by soldiers, and some half-dozen other patricians, including Gaius Caesar, Quintus Cicero, and Flaccus the praetor. One by one these shook hands with the condemned men, bidding them farewell, and I may say that never did I admire the five as then. Whatever their crimes, whatever their treason, at least they met their fate steadfastly and like Romans, and the craven Volturcius, whimpering and trembling in his home, might well envy them; life would assuredly hold no savor for me did I win it on such terms. Indeed, the five seemed less moved than those who bade them good-bye, and Cicero in particular wept openly and unashamed as he grasped their hands. Lentulus laid a hand on the consul's shoulder.

"Nay, my Tullius," he said, "grieve not so. It is what comes to every man, soon or late. The Gods have thus decreed. Farewell."

One by one the five were lowered into the Tullianum, then a half-dozen soldiers in charge of a centurion, and then the executioners. And as the trap-door closed over them a deep groan was wrenched from Cicero's bosom, his face twisted in convulsive grief, and leaning against the wall he wrapped the folds of his toga about his head to hide his features. Nervously Flaccus paced up and down; Cato stood with his face buried in his hands; and Quintus Cicero bit his nails to the very quick. Alone of all, Caesar stood calm, his countenance showing no trace of emotion, though I knew he was as deeply moved as any there. Verily, he had a mind and will of iron!

Presently there came a knock at the trap-door, and this was raised, a rope let down, and the centurion drawn up. Lifting his eyebrows in inquiry, Caesar glanced at the man, who saluted and bowed. Stepping across the room, Caesar laid his hand on Cicero's shoulder and spoke gently:

"Marcus."

Cicero dropped his toga, lifting a drawn and tear-stained face, and Caesar said:

"It is over."

The consul looked about for a moment, then said:

"I must not be seen thus." To the centurion: "Bring water."

Water was brought, and with his kerchief Cicero washed and dried his face. For perhaps half a minute he gazed at the floor, visibly struggling for composure, then at length he mastered himself and strode to the door, we others close behind.

As far as the eye could reach, the Comitium, the Forum, and the roofs were packed with a dense throng, and when Cicero appeared a great shout went up, to die away into silence as the consul raised his hand. When at last no sound came from that huge concourse he spoke, firm and unfaltering, in a voice that reached the utmost limits of the crowd:

"They have lived their lives."

And with even pace and steady eye, tall, dignified, a Roman to the core of his soul, the savior of Rome strode down the steps, across the Forum, and up the slope of the Palatine to his home.

CHAPTER X

Of the Battle of Pistorium; and the End of the Conspiracy

THE execution of the five had two instant effects. First, all alarm within the City was laid at rest, .for it was felt that with the death of these men the backbone of the conspiracy was broken. The streets took on an air of cheerfulness which had been for some time absent from them, business regained its normal state, and Cicero could not appear in public without being hailed with shouts of "Savior! Deliverer!" The other effect was no less important—indeed, it was more so—though not so immediately apparent. Ever since his flight, Catilina had been recruiting and training his army, and during the past week or ten days he had been marching slowly southward, drawing nearer the City so as to be within striking distance when the revolt within the walls, planned for the Feast of the Saturnalia, should take place. But with the death of the five and the flight of the other conspirators, it was plain that there would be no such outbreak, and Catilina began to withdraw from the neighborhood of Rome, retreating northward again.

A Slave of Catiline

Antonius the consul, with his troops, lay at Praeneste, and Quintus Metellus Celer, the praetor, was at Aesculum in the province of Picenum, ninety miles or so northeast of Rome, on the Via Salaria; the plan was that as soon as Catilina drew near the City, Antonius would interpose himself between the advancing army and Rome, while Celer, marching across country, would take the conspirators in the rear. But with the retreat of the invaders this plan was changed, for the opinion of military experts within the City was that Catilina would cross the mountains into Gallia Transalpina, and there foment rebellion. And since many of the Gallic tribes were by no means well affected toward Rome, this offered a serious danger; a leader from a patrician family—and a leader of influence and ability, at that —together with the nucleus of an army, might not incredibly set the whole of Gallia Transalpina in flame of rebellion. So Antonius was sent in pursuit, and Celer received orders to march with all speed into Etruria, and if possible head off the rebel retreat. Of the two, Antonius had the lighter task, having open country for his march, whereas Celer must lead his army through the passes of the Apennines, a thing not easy to do in winter.

The immediate danger of assassination being over, I was no longer in constant attendance on the consul, and one day about the Kalends of Januarius,

The End of the Conspiracy

Tullia, Tiro, and I were huddled about a charcoal brazier in the *atrium,* conversing and trying to keep warm. I was telling them of sundry adventures of my boyhood, of fishing trips I had made with my foster-father, and Tiro listened as eagerly as did the little girl; though educated, refined, and a delightful companion, he was not a man of action, so he thrilled to stories of rough adventure, as a student always does. We were interrupted by a slave, who said to me:

"The consul demands your presence."

Excusing myself to my hearers, I went at once to Cicero's office, where I found him just sealing a letter, pressing his signet-ring into the wax that bound the cord. He looked up as I entered.

"Ah, Tiberius," he said. "I have an errand for you—a long one. This letter is for Metellus Celer, who is, I understand, in the neighborhood of Faesulae. Find him and deliver these tablets, with all speed. Take from the stables whatever horse you choose; Automedon has orders to deliver the one you select. It will be best, I think, for you to go out by the Porta Flumentana and follow the Via Aurelia along the coast; otherwise you might fall into the hands of the rebels. However, be guided by your own judgment; the main thing is to get this message to Celer as quickly as the Gods permit."

237

I took the letter, bowed, and was turning to depart when he stopped me.

"One moment, Tiberius. It may be that you would like to stay for the fighting which will take place when the armies of the State meet Catilina. If so, there is no reason why you should not remain. Farewell."

Dismissed, I took my way to the stables, where Automedon bridled for me a sturdy, spirited black horse; and mounting, I rode out from the City. As the consul had suggested, I took the coast road to the north, turning over in my mind, as I went, Cicero's words.

Man is a strange animal! While in Dumnorix' school, I thought I had received my fill of fighting, thought I would never again wish to cross swords with anyone. The sight of men wounded and brought down by my hand was abhorrent to me, and I vowed that if ever I were freed from that slavery my fighting days were over. But now, a free man—or practically so—and under no obligation to draw my sword, I found the heart within my bosom glowing, felt my cheeks flush and my spirit leap at the prospect of going into battle. It is curious, but however reluctant a man may be to hurt another, there is yet in combat a fierce joy, an exaltation beyond anything else the world has to give. To feel the grind and rasp of an enemy's steel on yours, to see his eyes glaring at you over the rim of his shield, to know that he is bending all his powers to your destruction, that no one can help you, and that you must slay him or be yourself slain—earth has no such other mighty thrill, and I doubt if the heroes in the Elysian Fields know such joy. And long before I had crossed Tiber I knew that I would remain with the army.

It was early in the day when I set out, so I made a fairly good stage of about forty-five miles to Centum Cellae, where I lay that night. Doubtless had I been changing horses at post-houses I could have done better, but I must make one beast do for the whole journey, and further, being unused to riding, I wished to spare myself somewhat; I felt that thus I could in the end make better speed. As it was, I was lame enough when I set out next morning, but this lameness wore off in the course of an hour or so, and I did a little better the second day, halting for the night at a roadside inn some fifteen miles beyond Cosa.

Here I had an adventure which, though of no special importance, was yet amusing in a way. While eating my supper in the common room, I noticed a group of men who, in a corner, were drinking and listening to one of their number. He, apparently a rural gladiator, was boasting to his companions of his prowess, and they, youths of the neighborhood, drank in his wine and his boasts with equal enthusiasm. At length, intoxicated with his own words as much as with the wine, he must needs demonstrate his ability with weapons, and to that end selected me for victim. Swaggering over to where I sat, he opened on me with questions, from that passed to abuse, and when I failed to resent his words he spat out an oath and knocked the bowl of stew from my hands, spattering the food about the room, while his friends applauded loudly. Seeing that there was nothing else for it, I got to my feet, set my back against the wall, and drew my sword, as he drew his and advanced upon me. But my movement had brought my face into the firelight, which illumined my features and, I imagine, glinted on my red thatch. My assailant brought up as though jerked back by a rope, eyed my face and hair, saw that I held my sword in my left hand, and sheathed his own weapon with a haste that was ludicrous.

"I most humbly beg Your Honor's pardon," he said, obsequiously. "Had I known—had I suspected—that we were honored by the presence of Tiberius the Red I would not have dared. . . . I beg that Your Honor will graciously pardon my insolence and allow me to replace your supper, adding thereto a goblet of wine."

One of the youths in the corner laughed jeeringly,

and the gladiator turned on him so fierce a look that he fell silent.

"It is no disgrace to humble oneself before Tiberius of the school of Dumnorix," the swordsman told them. "I have seen him fight, and if any thinks I have disgraced myself—" A chorus of denial interrupted him, and the end of the affair was that I had no small trouble to escape to bed sober, so many were the goblets urged on me by the enthusiastic company.

The next day was the best of all my trip. I was getting up into the hills, and the road, skirting the coast, brought me often in sight of my beloved sea for, unlike most Romans, I have always been intensely fond of the ocean—doubtless because of my early life upon its bosom. At times the road bent inland, and then again, topping some rise of ground or skirting some rocky headland, I caught glimpses of the Mare Tyrrhenum, lying in its intense blue under the winter sky, or breaking in crested foam on the rocks far below me. I could see at times a low-lying dark mass which I knew to be Corsica, and twice I thrilled to small fishing-boats, like the one in which I had so often sailed, skimming along over the dark sea. The air stung in my nostrils like wine, my horse bore me strongly onward, and so joyous was I that more than once, finding myself alone upon the road, I sang. I am no musician, to be sure, but when there is none to criticize I can make sounds which please my own ear and keep time to the rolling thunder of a horse's gallop. All in all, it was a day to live in the memory, and though tired I was happy when at nightfall I turned aside from the main road to ride some four or five miles into Populonium.

The day following, I made a stage of fifty-five or sixty miles to Pisae, and here I learned that Metellus Celer was at Pistorium, some thirty-five miles beyond; Catilina, they told me, was at Faesulae, about fifteen miles southeast of where Celer awaited him. A battle was imminent, for Antonius was coming rapidly up from the south, and Catilina was trapped; Celer was blocking him off from Gallia, and Antonius from Rome, so there was nothing left for him to do but fight.

Late on the fifth day after leaving Rome, I rode into Celer's camp at Pistorium and made my way to the *praetorium,* where I delivered Cicero's letter to the general. He read it, then said to me:

"The consul says that you may wish to join my army. Is such the case?"

"If I may be permitted, General."

Nodding, he called a decurion and gave me into his charge, saying:

"See that he has arms, food, and a place to sleep.

Put him into the century of Decius Liber." And with a wave of his hand he dismissed me.

The decurion turned me over to a private soldier, who eyed me with some interest, finally asking:

"Are you not Tiberius the Red?"

"The same," I replied. It was being borne in upon me that I was a character of note!

"I saw you conquer Aulus Barbatus at Pompeii," he told me. "I was stationed there at the time, and served as one of the arena guards. *Mehercle,* what a fight! I yelled myself hoarse. Did you often fight as a Samnite?"

"Hardly ever. Generally as a *retiarius.*"

"Indeed! It is amazing that a *retiarius* should be so good with sword and shield. And now you are serving with us. Well, you will have a chance for more fighting; they say the rebels have sworn neither to give nor to take quarter." We had been threading our way through the camp while we talked, and now my guide stopped at one of the many fires. "Here is a friend of yours," he remarked to the group, and as they looked up one of them leaped to his feet with a shout and next moment Pugnax and I were in each other's arms.

Explanations followed, and I learned that my friend had been sent, with the century in which he had enlisted, to join Metellus Celer.

"And we shall have some good fighting, my Tiberius," he assured me. "Antonius joined us this afternoon, with a legion and a half, and Celer has as many. Catilina is at Faesulae, and cannot escape; we shall have a battle by to-morrow or next day, for certain."

"We heard in the City," I replied, "that Catilina's men were falling away from him, discouraged by the execution of the five and the failure of the revolt within the walls. Is there truth in the rumor?"

"*Per Martes!*" laughed one of the group. "There is, indeed! Our spies report that he has but half a legion remaining. Many have deserted to us, under promise of amnesty."

I whistled in astonishment.

"*Edepol!* Three thousand! And we have six times as many? It will be a massacre, not a battle."

"Do not think it," another spoke up. "The rebels are desperate, and will fight like cornered rats."

"But at such odds—"

"Personally," still another interrupted, "I am content that the odds are what they are. Three thousand desperate fighters—lost men—can do enough damage to satisfy any reasonable stomach, and I am prepared to thank the consul that Catilina has not the twelve thousand that he once had. He is a great man, this consul of ours."

The End of the Conspiracy

"Antonius?" inquired Pugnax, mischievously, and a general laugh went up.

"Antonius has the gout—or so he says," the first speaker commented. "Myself, I think the sickness is not of the feet, but of the heart."

The opinion of the soldiers seemed to be that Antonius was shamming illness because he was a coward, but I do not believe that this was true. He had always borne the reputation of being a brave man, he had served with distinction in the army, and I remembered hearing Lentulus tell Catilina that Antonius favored the conspiracy, so I am convinced that he avoided the battle in order not to be active against Catilina. How he could reconcile that with leading the forces of the State up to this point, I cannot tell; I merely believe that it was sympathy and not cowardice which held the consul in his tent when the battle joined.

For we had a battle. Two days after I reached Pistorium, the morning bugles blew us to attention, and we were instructed to arm and prepare for fighting. Marching out from camp, we were drawn up in battle array, and about the third hour the army of the conspirators came in sight, marching across country toward us. To me, who had seen nothing of warfare, they seemed a magnificent and imposing spectacle, but the veterans in our ranks grunted and swore their disgust at the ragged lines of the rebels.

Indeed, looking back, I can laugh at my own credulousness, for later, under Caesar, I learned what an army can be.

"Not but what Catilina has done wonders with them, in so short a time," remarked a grizzled centurion who stood near me. "To make anything but a rabble of such troops in two months is no small achievement. He is a good leader. Pity that he is fighting against the State."

"Part of the credit is due to Manlius," spoke up a decurion, and the centurion nodded.

"Gaius Manliu⸱ is a good man, too," he admitted. "I served under him, years ago. Well, boys, it will not be long that we shall have to wait."

And in truth the rebels were forming in line of battle some hundred paces from us. I could see the centurions passing along the front of their array, marshalling them in place; and gleaming in the early rays of the sun I saw the silver eagle that Catilina had sent, the famous eagle that once was carried before the legions of Gaius Marius. And now Catilina himself rode out before his men, exhorting them, encouraging them to do their utmost, and though it was too far for me to make out his words, I could hear the well-remembered tones of his voice ringing sweet and musical over the frosty fields. A pang of grief shot through me that I must fight against him, for even admitting that he was a traitor to the State, and deserved the punishment which had been meted out to Lentulus and the others, yet, by all the Gods, he was a fine man—and I loved him.

Petreius, lieutenant-general to Antonius, and a brave and gallant leader, rode out and exhorted us, and a deep-chested shout acknowledged the inspiration of his words. And now the rebel bugles blew the charge, and the enemy line surged forward into motion.

"Stand to it, men!" shouted our centurions. "For Rome and the Hearth of Vesta! Stand firm!"

Breaking into a trot, and from that into a run, with gradually increasing speed the rebel line bore down upon us. So eager were both sides to come to grips that no javelins were hurled, but with a roar of voices and a crash of steel the battle joined.

How to describe that dreadful mêlée? Poets and writers claim to tell the course of a battle, but for myself—and others, I find, are like me—I can see nothing of the whole affair, but have only a series of small pictures stamped upon my brain. My attention is so concentrated that a dense fog closes me in on both sides, and I see only what is directly before me. I recall taking blows on my shield, parrying and thrusting, and I can remember some who confronted me, notably a giant who wore a

slave-collar about his neck and bore the word *fur* *
branded on his forehead. Also, a broad-shouldered,
thick-set man whom I knew for Aulus Gabinius, a
gladiator whom I had seen in the arena at Ravenna.
The former succumbed easily to a feint at the eyes
and a cut to the leg, but Gabinius had more skill in
fence, and held me in play for several minutes
before I got past his guard. And I recall stabbing
a man who lifted his sword over Pugnax' head
while my friend's attention was given to another
assailant. For the rest, I have only a confused
memory of a number of duels, of shouts, oaths,
groans, and the clash of steel, until at length I
found myself unopposed, and looking about I saw
that the battle was nearly over; only a handful still
offered resistance.

A glance at the sun told me that we had been
fighting for a little more than an hour, and suddenly I realized that I was tired and passionately
thirsty. All up and down our line the ground was
strewn with bodies, those of rebels and legionaries
lying together in heaps and windrows, and there was
no pursuit; each rebel died in his place, and each
and every one bore all his wounds in front; wrong-
headed though they were, it must be acknowledged
that they were brave.

But my eye was caught by a knot of men some

* Thief.

"TIBERIUS, I ALWAYS LOVED YOU. . . . THIS
SHOULD WIN YOUR FREEDOM. . . . FAREWELL."

distance back from the line of battle, fully thirty paces to our rear. They stood about, gazing at something on the ground, and with curiosity roused, I made my way thither. Pushing through the crowd, I saw Catilina lying on his back, his head pillowed on the body of a soldier. The rebel leader's helmet was off, his armor was hacked and cut, his broken sword lay beside him, and he was bleeding from a score of wounds. All about him lay the bodies of legionaries whom he had brought down in his last desperate charge deep into our ranks, but I paid them no heed. Dropping on my knees with a cry of distress, I seized his hand, and whether at the sound or the touch, he opened his eyes.

"Ha, Tiberius!" he greeted me, faintly. "It is you again. . . . I had thought that of all, you at least would be faithful to me. . . ."

"*Domine,*" I cried in agony, "I was until you planned to slay the consul. But for that I would be lying beside you now. That, though, I could not stomach. Forgive me!"

I felt his hand press mine feebly.

"It is forgiven . . ." he said. "You were a good servant until then . . . each must follow his conscience . . . it was a mistake . . . like others I have made. . . ."

"*Domine,*" I cried again, "let me stanch your wounds. You may yet—"

The End of the Conspiracy

He smiled and shook his head, and for a moment his strength flared up a trifle.

"Charon beckons," he murmured. "It is better so. I have no mind to go as did Lentulus and the others. I shall soon meet them . . . take my greetings to the consul . . . Cicero . . . and to Sempronia . . . the Gods be with you, Tiberius . . . I always loved you . . . this should win your freedom . . . farewell. . . ." His hand clutched mine, he shivered slightly, relaxed, lay still, while the salt tears streamed down my cheeks and fell on his upturned face. And thus on the field of battle passed Lucius Sergius Catilina, patrician, leader, and rebel. His fitting epitaph was written by one who afterward told of his deeds: "A most beautiful death, had he but fallen while fighting for, rather than against, his country."

But little remains to tell. Gaius Manlius and Publius Furius died in the battle, but some few of Catilina's men, escaping from the field, threw themselves into the fastnesses of the Etrurian hills, and there continued a futile resistance, under command of one Lucius Sergius, a freedman of Catilina's. But their resistance was a matter of weeks only, and in the end Celer hunted them down and stamped out the final embers of the conspiracy. Some others of the conspirators, being taken, were executed, and still others lived in exile, their goods being confiscated to the State. Sempronia and Fulvia were ignored by the authorities; Rome does not war on women.

Back once more in the City, I received the formal thanks of the Senate for saving the life of the consul. My mother acknowledged me publicly as her son, and to make my inheritance secure, went through the formality of legal adoption, whereupon, my father being dead, I became the head of the house of Rufus, a branch of the Cornelian gens, and one of the proudest and wealthiest families of Rome. And I believe I am the only patrician in all the City who can show pierced ears and a scourge-marked back to prove the fickleness of the goddess Fortuna.

Some question was raised as to the ownership of Pugnax, Fulvia claiming that Curius had given him to her. Curius was in exile, and Pugnax could claim freedom under the edict, but as the simplest and surest way of settling the matter I gave Fulvia twenty *sestertia* for a bill of sale, and Pugnax was made over to me. I bought Polla at the same time, and promptly manumitted them both before the praetor; they were married from my home on the Palatine, and few patricians boasted a more gorgeous wedding than could this freedman and his bride. My mother took an instant liking to Polla, took her under protection, and I furnished the money to set Pugnax up in business. He having a taste for weapons, I rented a booth in the Forum and a forge outside the wall, but from the business of armorer he branched out into various investments in salt-mines, tax-farming, and the like, with such success that in about fifteen years he could show the requisite five hundred *sestertia,* and receiving citizenship, assumed equestrian rank. His oldest son bears the name of Tiberius Cornelius Rufus Pugnax.

For twenty years, up to the time of the ex-consul's death, I remained intimate with Cicero, and I am proud to say that even during the stormy years of the Civil War, when he was at odds with Caesar and I was serving with the latter, I was able to keep on friendly terms with both those leaders. And I thank the Immortal Gods that in Their kindness They have permitted me to know intimately the man who was Rome's greatest orator and one of the most devoted statesmen and noblest souls this world has ever seen, Marcus Tullius Cicero.

AUTHOR'S NOTE

IN writing this Author's Note, I cannot do better than quote the words of a far more able writer than myself, namely, Winston Churchill: "The reality of the foregoing pages has to the author at least, become so vivid that he regrets the necessity of having to add an afterword. Every novel is, to some extent, a compound of truth and fiction, and he has done his best to picture conditions as they were, and to make the spirit of his book true."

One exception may be made to this last sentence It would not be desirable, in a book of this type, to dwell on one of the most conspicuous characteristics of Cicero's era—the fact that, judged by our modern ideals, the average Roman noble was extremely lax in moral standards. Customs vary with the years, what is proper or at least excusable in one century being severely condemned in the next, and it is sufficient to bear in mind that there were some men, notably Cicero, Cato, and—in his later life— Caesar, whose morals would be thought rigid even in our own time.

There will be some to quarrel with my portrait of Catiline. But we must remember that the accepted picture of this man is given us by his foes, and that political enmities in Rome were bitter beyond anything that we know, regarding the most outrageous personal abuse as a legitimate weapon.

Author's Note

Unquestionably, he was a traitor to the State, but an unsuccessful rebel against constituted authority is always a traitor; if successful, he becomes in the eyes of history a noble and high-minded patriot. And even Catiline's enemies agree that he was a man of great courage and great personal charm.

There is some difference of opinion among authorities regarding the age of Cicero's children at the time of the conspiracy, and I have elected to follow the ones whose statements best fit the purpose of the story. Thanks are due Miss Lillian Lowell, of the East Orange High School, for information on this point, as well as for other suggestions and for criticism.

Strictly classical minds may object to some phrases which I have used, but it should be remembered that the Romans were as much given to slang as we are to-day, and the casual language of a gladiator was no more that of Cicero's orations than the speech of a modern prizefighter is that of Addison and Macaulay.

I have committed a slight anachronism in making Tiberius quote, in his description of Catiline's death, an author whom he could not have known. But the words so excellently characterize not only Catiline's death but—in spirit, at least—his entire political life, that I may be excused for including them.

P. L. A.

East Orange, New Jersey.